ANY JOB WILL DO

BOOK ONE OF THE GRAND HUMAN EMPIRE

JOHN WILKER

Ryan,
Help! I'm trapped
in a chewing gum
factory! :)
Enjoy!

EDITED BY
CHRISTINA SHORT

Rogue Publishing

Cover art by: Vivid Covers

V 3

ISBN: 978-1-951964-05-4

CONTENTS

I can't thank my wife, Nicole enough for supporting me in this adventure!

You're about to embark on a fun adventure!

When you're done reading, I hope you'll take a minute to leave a review!

If you liked the story and want more, joining my newsletter is a great way to get free samples, and exclusive short stories.

If you like supporting things you love by sporting merch or buying direct, well you're in luck! I've launched a shop, take a look. **Use, discount code "Osprey" and you'll save %15!**

PART ONE

ONE

HOW IT ALWAYS STARTS

"Attention, unregistered vessel." The voice came over the overhead speaker. "You have violated restricted space. Prepare to reverse course and return to Orbital Twelve."

Jax reached over and flipped the switch, shutting the comm system off. "Dumb conversation." He pushed the throttle control closer to the top. The nimble Valerian Co-op Infiltrator lurched a bit as her powerful engines roared.

"They are locking weapons." The ceiling speaker announced. Skip, the ship's managing intelligence, intoned. A warning tone sounded.

Jax pushed, pulled, and twisted the flight controls, sending the small craft into a series of erratic maneuvers. The target lock tone fell silent.

"See." He said.

The tone returned.

"Yes." Skip replied.

Jax growled and checked the small tactical readout. Three Imperial corvettes were converging on his location; two from orbit near the station he just left, not really a threat. The third, however, was coming from outside the gravity well of the planet. It was a threat.

"Welp, this is how we go out, I guess." Rudy said.

Jax didn't acknowledge him. Instead, he adjusted their course again, bringing them into a direct collision course with the oncoming imperial corvette.

"Captain..." Skip said.

The weapons lock alert got louder. Through the transparent titanium view screen, the Imperial ship was getting larger and larger.

"Jackson..." Rudy whined.

Moments before collision, Jax threw the flight controls hard over while mashing a foot down on one of the pedals below the console. The lithe ship twisted and shot under the much larger vessel with barely twenty meters between them. The two ships shields touched, causing both to glow orange as they ground against each other.

The moment the two ships parted, the weapon's lock tone silent, Jax powered up the wormhole generator.

In minutes the small ship was billions of kilometers away, racing through a wormhole.

NOT ALL JOBS ARE GOOD JOBS

"I wish you'd consult me on these jobs. Carrying contraband will get me impounded," Skip said from the speaker in the ceiling. The Valerian Co-op Infiltrator was still hurtling through the compressed space time of a wormhole. The low hum of the wormhole generator down in Engineering vibrated through the ship.

Jackson Caruso, Jax to his friends, was back sitting at the pilot station. They had been traveling for five hours, Jax had taken a nap. He looked up. "Oh, come on. It's not like this is the first job like this that we've done. It's always fine. You worry too much." He grinned. He consulted his console. The cargo hold two decks below had several containers that were almost certainly full of something highly illegal.

"Easy for you to say. The Empire won't scrap you and reformat your brain over and over until you're dead."

From one of the two stations behind Jax's pilot station, Rudy, a small, rust-colored navigation droid said, "And turn your body into a toaster or dishwasher."

"For an SI you're awfully melodramatic. Have I ever

told you that?" He looked over his shoulder to Rudy. "Both of you." Computer intelligences fell into two categories: sentient intelligence (SI) and rudimentary intelligence (RI). Skip and Rudy were both of the former variety. RIs tended to be nav computers, strategy assistants, and the like. Things that didn't speak and usually had only a single function. SIs ran households, ships, cities, and such. Or at least they did before the Empire.

Skip was the SI that managed the systems of the *Osprey*, Jax's Scout Ship. He got his name from Jax as a toddler. Jax's parents had just addressed the SI as "ship," but when Jax was learning to speak, *ship* came out *skip*, and it stuck.

From the speakers, there was a static crackle. Then Skip said, "Twenty seconds to normal space."

From his station, Rudy said, "According to the contract, we're to meet up with a freighter to offload the cargo."

"Five, four, three, two," Skip began counting down. When he hit *one*, the swirling purple-hued vortex the ship was in flashed, and a pitch-black void opened directly ahead of them. In the span of a heartbeat, the *Osprey* was back in normal space.

"One contact, fifty thousand kilometers out and closing," Skip announced.

"Must be our contact," Rudy said. He disconnected from his station. Jax's parents had modified it when they bought Rudy. Technically, Skip could do navigation calculations on his own. Rudy, however, had specialized processing cores and could run the calculations faster. Every second had made a difference in the war. His cylindrical body had a single smart material rollerball that he balanced on. Jax always teased him that he looked like an upside-down deodorant stick with arms. He rolled forward to stop next to Jax's seat. "Ugly." He raised a thin metal arm, pointing out the transparent forward windows.

Now less than twenty thousand kilometers and closing off their port bow was a freighter at least a dozen times bigger than the *Osprey*. Where the Valerian Co-op Infiltrator was sleek and aerodynamic, the freighter was a massive rectangle with engines. The crew and command module made up a spine that ran from the engines forward. Cargo modules were connected to that spine at hardpoints. Jax couldn't see a single module that didn't look older than him. The freighter had closed the gap to less than a kilometer and was still approaching.

Jax nodded. "No kiddin'." He looked at his console. A light was blinking. He tapped the communications controls, then looked at one of the monitors mounted above his station. A middle-aged woman appeared. Jax smiled. "Hi there, I'm—"

She held up a hand. "I don't need to know your name. You have the cargo?"

Jax nodded. "Yup. How do you want to do this?" Under his breath he mumbled, "Rude."

"Fast. Pull alongside. Drift the cargo over."

Jax groaned as quietly as he could. "Sounds like a plan." The screen flickered, then resumed showing a schematic of the *Osprey*. He looked at the ceiling. "Baxter, we're drifting the cargo over. You good to take care of that?" He looked out the forward window, the ugly freighter was now just over a hundred meters away.

A groan sounded from the ceiling speakers. "Yeah."

DO THE JOB YOU'RE PAID TO DO

Down in the cargo hold of the *Osprey,* a matte black combat droid was shoving two meter by two meter cargo modules around, moving them closer to the portside cargo door. Wirelessly, he instructed Skip, *Kill the gravity, please.*

A second later, everything in the not-overly-large cargo hold shifted as the artificial gravity disengaged. Baxter, a Mark IX combat droid, magnetized his feet, then asked Skip to open the cargo door. When the thick door slid away, he saw the much larger bulk freighter parked less than one hundred meters away from the *Osprey.* An equally large cargo door slid open on the other vessel, revealing two crewmen in bulky EVA suits. One of them waved. Their gloves were not the same color as the rest of their suit.

Baxter returned the gesture, then guided the first of ten modules across. It would be nice to have room to move in the cargo hold again. As it moved through the static atmosphere barrier that kept the ship's atmosphere inside, a faint blue line moved across it. Seeing as he could vaporize a small rodent from over a kilometer away with any of his assorted blasters, drifting a two-ton cargo module a hundred meters to arrive exactly where he wanted without crushing the parties on the receiving end was a piece of cake. In less than ten minutes, Baxter had sent all ten modules across to the other ship. He didn't wait for the last one to be caught by the other ship as he closed the cargo door. *We're good to go,* he wirelessly transmitted to the flight deck.

On the flight deck, Baxter's voice came out of the overhead speakers. "We're good to go."

Jax nodded and toggled the comm system. "We're heading out, unless you need anything else."

The woman appeared on the screen again. "We're all set. I've let our contact know that we've made the hand off." She made a mock salute gesture, then closed the channel.

Jax powered up the sub-light engines and guided the *Osprey* away from the larger cargo hauler. "Wormhole generator ready?" he asked.

From his station, Rudy answered, "Yup, board is green."

Humanity had been trying to unlock the secrets of Faster Than Light travel for decades when the solution fell into their laps. While most of the United Nations was working on Alcubierre Warp Drive technology, a small Japanese expedition to the Jovian moon Ganymede discovered the ruins of a crashed starship, alien in every way. Aboard the ship was a functional wormhole generator. Once scientists found out what it was, it took less than twenty years to reverse engineer and mass produce human made versions. The owners of the ship never showed up, and no ship like the Ganymede ship was ever seen again, anywhere.

The galactic gold rush began the moment the first colony transport went through the swirling energy vortex of a wormhole bound for the Alpha Centauri System, then

Epsilon Eridani, Wolf 359, and so on. Humanity spread quickly from then on.

Once Jax had confirmed that the wormhole was stable, he powered down the flight console, letting Skip take over. "Two days back to Kelso. I'm gonna reheat that pizza and watch some TV." He went down the stairs.

ARE YOU JACKSON CARUSO?

The *Angry Spacer* was the type of place that visitors to Kelso station would hear about, then stay as far away from as possible—which was what made it Jax Caruso's favorite, or at least second favorite, place on the station. His favorite was probably his mechanical bay. After Skip, it was the only thing he owned. Memaw left him the bay when she passed. After his parents were killed, she had raised him for a few years before a rare cancer that medical science couldn't cure took her.

Lucas wiped the bar in front of Jax with a rag that seemed to apply dirt, not remove it. His cybernetic arm whirred and clicked as it moved. "Haven't seen you in a bit, Jax." He placed a tall glass of beer on the bar and pushed it towards Jax's open hand.

Jax nodded, dropping onto a barstool. "Picked up a courier job, ended up running who knows what out to the Neo Egypt sector." He looked around. "You haven't seen the Delphinos, have ya?"

Lucas shook his head, his arm whirring as he grabbed a

bottle of something pink from the shelf. "Nope, haven't seen 'em in a few days."

Jax smiled. "Good. I owe 'em money and don't think Stevie can keep Marshmallow from kicking my ass for much longer."

"You know what would keep him from kicking your butt? Paying them. Course, whatever is going on with you and Steve may be complicating that," the other man offered before nodding to a group of spacers that might have been natives of the Neo Egypt sector themselves.

"Where's the fun in that?" Jax replied loud enough for Lucas to still hear. The other man shook his head as he approached the ebony-skinned spacers.

"Are you Jackson Caruso?" a voice asked from behind him.

Jax didn't look up. "Nope."

He looked over his shoulder at a middle-aged white man in what looked like an expensive suit. It took the man a few seconds before he said, "Uh, your business manager said I'd find you here and described you, in detail."

Jax shrugged. "He's a liar."

"So, you are Jackson Caruso?" the man pressed.

Jax exhaled and spun on his barstool. "What do you want? I have a lovely night of getting drunk and making questionable decisions ahead of me." He turned slightly to catch the eye of a woman sitting with two friends at a table a dozen or two feet from the bar. He winked. The woman blushed while her two friends had what would at best be highly disapproving expressions on their faces.

The business man cleared his throat. "Um, yes, well, I need your help. I'm Sylvester Kline. I represent ReliefCorp. We'd like to hire you."

Jax looked around. He leaned over to look behind the

businessman for the candid vidcast crew that surely was lurking nearby. "Uh, what? Why would you want to me to be a relief worker? Nothing in my life would make anyone think that was a thing I'd excel at."

From the other end of the bar, Lucas said, "Yeah, he's pretty selfish." Jax looked down the length of the bar and flipped him off. Lucas added, "And lazy." The bartender smirked.

The man cleared his throat. "I...no." He shook his head. "We don't want you as a relief worker. We need you to rescue some, actually."

Jax turned back to the businessman. "I'm sorry, what? Rescue them? The aid workers?"

The man pushed Jax aside to set a data tablet on the bar. The screen came to life showing a data file for a planet, Mariposa.

"Mariposa?" Jax asked, "The bloody-civil-war-in-progress Mariposa?"

Kline looked from the tablet to Jax. "Well, yes, currently. ReliefCorp has had an aid station set up in the lower highlands outside the capital for almost five years. We've been helping build out their infrastructure. The Imperial supported government has been making strides in consolidating their control over the planet. Our camp was helping those efforts. We'd assembled several large solar farms to bring power to the capital and several outlying settlements."

Jax blinked. "And..."

Kline sighed. "Three weeks ago, we lost contact with the camp. We believe the comm sat, left in orbit when the workers were dropped off, has been destroyed."

Jax tapped the tablet screen, scrolling the data. "So have

the Empire take care of it. They want the planet, after all. Their puppet government is in control, right?"

"Well, we would, but," the man cleared his throat again, looking incredibly uncomfortable, "the Imperials pulled out just over a week ago." Jax opened his mouth, but Kline continued, "Apparently, whatever the Empire was hoping to get out of having Mariposa under their control didn't pan out, so they left. Took their equipment, their troops, all of it. Without the Imperial presence, things have quickly spun out of control. The rebels launched full-scale attacks on several cities. There is fighting in the streets of the capital. One of the settlements nearby has been completely destroyed."

Jax nodded slowly. "I see, and so, what? You want me to go grab your do-gooders, yeah?" Kline nodded. Jax continued, "And my, *business manager,* gave you our standard contract?"

Again, Kline nodded, "He did, yes." He reached over and tapped the tablet, and a copy of Jax's typical contract appeared. He had paid a middling amount to someone he thought was probably a lawyer to draw up the boilerplate agreement.

Jax picked up the tablet, then tapped the earpiece he kept in his ear almost all the time. "Rudy?"

"Yeah, boss?" the voice on the other end replied.

"This contract good?"

"Yeah, they made a few tweaks, added names of the people they want to make sure to get back, where to drop them off, but otherwise, all good." There was a pause. "The money is good, too."

Jax grunted and placed his thumb on the sensor at the lower corner of the tablet. He looked up at Mr. Kline. "I'll leave in an hour." He handed the tablet back to the man.

"That's great news, Captain Caruso, thank you." Kline grabbed his data tablet and backed away.

Jax looked over to where Lucas was standing. "One more." He picked up his barely touched glass and downed its content in only a few large gulps.

TWO

OFF WE GO

The mechanical bay was only slightly larger than the *Osprey*. In one corner, Jax had arranged a makeshift living room complete with a couch of questionable provenance and a wall-mounted entertainment screen. A refrigerator sat nearby full of takeout from various food stalls and beer. In the opposite corner sat a small office. Before the cancer took her, Memaw did business out of it. Jax never knew what that business was other than being a founding member of the collective that built Kelso station.

Jax pulled his gPhone out of a pocket on his worn leather jacket. He tapped the screen showing the *Osprey's* key systems. "Rudy, Skip. Let's get pre-flights started."

Between the *Osprey* and the mechanical bay, everything Jax owned was in one place. His grandmother had left him the bay when she died. It had been in the family since the station came online. It was Memaw's, then his parents', and now it was his.

"Acknowledged, Captain," Skip said. The boarding hatch on the ship lowered, and the ramp flipped down, allowing access.

Before Jax could reach the ramp, an upside-down roller-ball deodorant stick rolled down the ramp. Jax looked at the droid. "Business manager?"

The rust-colored droid rolled over next to Jax. Since it didn't have shoulders, it just moved both arms out into V shapes. "The guy asked who I was. I figured '*navigation droid*' wouldn't have impressed him." The droid fell in behind Jax, rolling next to him as he walked over to the bundle of wires and tubes plugged into the main trunk connection port under the *Osprey,* between the two leg-like landing gear the ship balanced on.

Jax shrugged. "Yeah, probably." He turned to the droid that came up only to his waist. "You're lucky the money was good."

Rudy rolled backward a foot. "Sorry I ruined your planned night of drinking too much and making question-able sexual choices." He rolled further back when Jax tried to kick him.

Jax said, "Skip, anything to worry about?"

From the small commset in his ear, Jax heard the ship's reply. "Not really. I mean, the list of things you need to fix hasn't changed, so there's that. There's nothing on the repair list that will hamper doing the job."

Jax nodded. "Okay, let's head out."

As he and Rudy reached the ramp, the bundle of tubes and wiring disconnected, falling to the floor before being automatically retracted into the wall of the bay. Rudy spun his squat, cylindrical head to look at the trunk lines now pulling toward the wall, something brown and runny spilling out of one of the tubes. "You know, this bay wouldn't smell so bad if you'd disconnect the trunk lines yourself instead of letting them hit the floor like that."

Jax got to the top of the ramp and looked back at his

small mechanical friend. "Yeah, but then I'd get that shit all over me."

Rudy sighed as he cleared the threshold to the small boarding area, the ramp folding as it rose. He moved to the staircase that led up to the decks above. The center of the circular staircase was empty and just big enough for Rudy to enter. By controlling the ship's artificial gravity within the slim column, Rudy could zip between decks with ease. He left Jax behind as he headed up.

"Skip, get us cleared for departure," Jax said as he headed up the stairs.

By the time he got to the next deck, taking in the mostly empty cargo hold, Skip said, "We're cleared for departure, Jax."

"Be right up," Jax said, rounding the corner to take the stairs up.

The flight deck of the *Osprey* wasn't that big. Not that it mattered to Jax, since it was just him and the droids. He didn't enjoy having people around, let alone up on the flight deck. He dropped into the forward pilot station and looked out the wrap around transparent view port. He turned to look at Rudy, who had plugged himself into the portside crew station. "Ready?"

The droid's head swiveled. "Yup."

Several orange strobe lights began flashing as the mechanical bay outer doors slid apart. "That view doesn't get old," Jax said, staring out at the black of space beyond the mechanical bay. As the heavy doors slid apart, a blue outline became visible just beyond them. The static atmosphere shield kept air in but let ships, and people, if they wanted to, pass right through. A marvel of science. Pre-Empire science.

WELCOME TO MARIPOSA

"Exiting wormhole now," Jax said as the countdown on his console hit zero and the *Osprey* exited the wormhole she had been traveling through for three days. They were still trillions of kilometers from the planet Mariposa, near the outer planets. Mariposa was a dot not easily distinguishable from the surrounding stars.

"You don't need to announce it, you know." Skip said. Jax made a face.

Rudy rolled away from his station. "We're about ten hours from orbit."

Jax turned his chair around. "Skip, you got the helm?"

"Of course, I do. I have the helm even when you're sitting at the controls," the ship's SI replied.

"Okay, that's a little rude," Jax said from the top of the stairs.

"You're a horrible pilot," the ship replied, "and you don't repair dents when you cause them."

"I'm going to bed," Jax said, leaving the flight deck.

An alarm screamed through Jax's quarters, causing him to damn near levitate out of his bed. "Wha—what's wrong?" He rolled and fell out of bed, landing in a pile of discarded clothes.

The alarm stopped, and the lights came on. Skip said, "Nothing is wrong. We're about ten minutes from orbit."

Jax sat up, still on the floor. "You needed to sound an alarm for that?"

"No, but it was funny," the speaker in the ceiling replied.

When Jax opened the hatch to his quarters, he ran into a wall of matte black combat droid. He nearly fell backward. "Damn, Bax. What're you doing?" Jax asked.

The droid looked down. "I wanted to hear you fall out of your bed." The droid stepped aside so Jax could pass. "You were right, Skip, that was funny."

"Never gets old," the speaker in the corridor's ceiling replied.

"I hate you both, stupid metal heads," Jax said. He stopped by the small kitchenette and grabbed a beer from the fridge, checking the time on his gPhone to ensure it wasn't too early in the day for a drink. As he entered the flight deck from the stairwell, he said, "Skip, you have the coordinates for the camp?"

"Rudy sent them over, we're on target. Do you want to take over?" the SI asked as Jax sat down in the pilot's chair.

Jax dropped his beer into a cupholder he had bolted to the console. As he grabbed the flight controls, he said, "Yeah, I'll take over." He looked over his shoulder to where Rudy was plugged into his console. "Keep an eye out. I know the Imps pulled out, but I'm guessing someone still has air- or space monitoring." He added, "Anyone trying to talk to us?"

"Roger, Roger," Rudy quipped.

Skip said, "Not a peep. I'm picking up chatter here and there, but looks like whoever decided the aid workers didn't need a comm satellite also decided no one else did. There aren't many in orbit." He added, "Lot of debris, though."

The *Osprey* entered the atmosphere with a lurch, her shields angled to deflect as much of the atmosphere as possible. Plasma streamers formed along the forward shields. As the small scout vessel pushed deeper into the atmosphere, she rattled and bumped. Jax grabbed his beer and took a long pull before driving the ship hard to starboard so they'd overfly the target area from high up. "Wonder what the Imps wanted with this place. Scrub and grassland as far as the eye can see."

Rudy offered, "I think that's what the Imperials wanted. According to the WikiGalaxia, most of Mariposa's landmass is immensely arable. The colony is only ten years old, so they've only really settled about a thirtieth of the planet. Given another few decades, this planet should be capable of feeding a significant portion of the Empire." After a slight pause, "Assuming they don't annihilate themselves first."

Jax nodded, watching the ground approach as the *Osprey* descended. The aid camp was just becoming visible in a valley a few kilometers from the capital. As they overflew the capitol, he said, "Damn, that's bigger than I thought it'd be." What the capital lacked in skyscrapers it made up for in sprawl. The city was easily two kilometers wide. "I mean, jeez, is it windy here or something? These people afraid of heights?" The results of fighting were clear throughout the mid-sized city. Several buildings were engulfed in flames. A few had collapsed. There were not a lot of civilians visible on the streets.

Rudy replied, "Also according to WikiGalaxia, there are

three major metropolitan areas on Mariposa. The capital, Darby City, has a population of just over a million. It is the largest of the three cities." The droid consulted the *Osprey's* scanner data. "That might not be the case for long if the fighting continues like that." An explosion on the opposite side of the city belched fire and smoke into the sky. Several hovercraft veered away in different directions, many of them exchanging weapons fire as they separated.

Jax grunted, "Well, looks like right now the fighting is on the other side of town. Bax, prep the hold for guests, please."

From the overhead speaker, the matte black combat droid replied, "On it."

With the city falling behind them, Jax took the *Osprey* in a low flyover of the camp. "Looks like that field over there is the best bet for landing." He pointed out the window at a section of flattened earth at the outer edge of the camp. Someone had made a wobbly edged circle in white paint. The *Osprey* would fit but would likely cause some damage to the nearby structures. He could see the camp occupants beginning to mill around. Several were pointing at the aggressively angled Scout Ship getting closer and closer to their camp.

SPACE PEACE CORPS

As the boarding ramp lowered and unfolded, Jax walked down so that he was stepping off it the moment the ramp settled. He looked around, seeing a group of a half-dozen people approaching. They were shielding their faces from the minor dust storm the landing thrusters had kicked up. "Skip, stay hot. We're not gonna be on the ground long."

"Roger that," the ship replied.

When Jax was within shouting distance, he asked, "Who's in charge here?" Several of the aid workers looked around at each other. Jax added, "I don't actually care. I'm here to get you off-planet. Come with me if you want to live."

After a minute of awkward silence and rapid eye blinking from the group, a stunning young woman approached. "Who are you?" she shouted, hand on hip. Her jet-black hair was pulled back in a single braid. She was in cargo shorts and a white button-down shirt, sleeves buttoned at the wrists.

Jax kept walking until he was next to her. "Name's Jackson. I'm here to get you all out of here. The fighting is getting worse. Your organization wants you off-planet." He nodded to her shirt. "Aren't you hot?" He was in his usual going-ashore attire, dark brown canvas trousers and linen shirt with a utility vest over it. Folks sometimes made fun of his vest, until he produced the tool they were looking for, or a snack, or in a pinch, his flask. This time he was always sporting his sunglasses. Mariposa's star was bright.

"What? Like I should be in a bikini or something, it's just so hot out?" she asked, then added, "What do you mean, off-planet?"

Jax made a face, holding both hands up, palms out. "Woah, I just meant that you're in long sleeves. You know what? Never mind. As to the other thing, it's two words, or rather, one word hyphenated, I guess. Which one was confusing?" He made a hand gesture, his hand flat in front of his chest, then raised it as he moved it across his body. "Have you not realized you're cut off? From like, everything?"

By then she had led them away from the *Osprey* and into camp. It was a mix of tents and slightly more permanent looking canvas structures. The two were surrounded by the almost two dozen people of the camp. She frowned. "We assumed the comm satellite had malfunctioned. It's done that before. Why does ReliefCorp want us to leave?" An explosion echoed through the valley; black smoke rose over a nearby hill. Two dots raced up into the sky, banked and headed off in another direction.

Jax pointed over the hill to the black smoke smudging the sky. "Civil war..."

A tall, skinny man approached. "Naomi, what's going on? We're leaving?" He removed a pair of glasses and rubbed the lenses with his dirty t-shirt.

Naomi looked at the newcomer, then Jax, and back. "No, Martin, we're not leav—"

Jax interrupted, "Yes, Martin. You are leaving." He looked at Martin, then the group that had followed them from the landing area back into camp and grown by almost a dozen. "Pack your shit, take only what you can carry. The *Osprey* isn't that big. Grab your personal effects and head for my— "

Naomi held a hand up. "Excuse me." She glared at Jax. "We need to discuss this."

A flush began creeping up Jax's cheeks. He shook his head. "No time for committee meetings, sorry." He reached into a thigh pocket on his trousers, pulling out a small data tablet. "Here." He handed Naomi the device. Jax noticed that it turned on before she tapped the screen to wake it.

She scanned the screen: scrolled, scowled, scrolled some more, scowled some more. She lowered the device and looked at Martin as she offered it to him. "I guess we're leaving. Everyone, do as this guy says." She hitched a thumb at Jax.

Martin scanned the tablet. "Uh, yes, do as he says. It looks like ReliefCorp has recalled us."

From the earpiece in Jax's ear, Rudy said, "Jax, I've been listening to the local comms. Sounds like there's some sporadic fighting nearby. The militia is following a group of rebels heading this way. It might get close."

Jax nodded. "Copy that, stay on top of it." The comms clicked, so he knew Rudy acknowledged. He looked at the mostly still-standing-around aid workers. "Move your asses!" he barked. Everyone scrambled. He looked at Naomi, eyebrow raised. She moved to follow her colleagues, Martin in tow. He turned and started toward the *Osprey,* still unsure who was in charge of these folks, but certain he didn't like the bossy black haired woman.

Five minutes later, the first of the aid workers were filing toward the field where the *Osprey* was parked. Jax waved them toward the waiting ship. He tapped his earpiece. "Baxter, help get our guests situated. It's gonna be a tight fit."

"Copy that, boss," the deep voice of the combat droid replied.

Naomi walked up to Jax. "Everyone else is packing up. We haven't gotten ahold of Ingrid, though." She looked up at the ship. *Did her eyes just flicker?* "Valerian Co-op Infiltrator, model five."

"Who's Ingrid? Why do I care?" He met her eye. "Good eye. *Osprey's* been in the family a long time." He looked over her shoulder at the few stragglers still heading for the *Osprey*. "There are reports of fighting nearby." Something not very far away exploded, the fireball visible over a low rise. He shrugged. "Maybe she's dead."

Naomi didn't even flinch. She turned, pointing. "I think she went to the solar farm. The static discharge vanes play havoc with our local comms." She turned. "Come on, space boy."

"I think I'm probably older than you," he said, falling into step.

"Debatable." She didn't slow down. In fact, she moved into an easy jog.

As he ran, he tapped his earpiece. "Skip, keep the engines running and be ready on weapons."

"Copy that, boss," the ship replied.

SOLAR FARM FUN

The solar farm spread out for nearly a kilometer in concentric circles and resembled a metal forest. Each articulating collector sprouted thin metal filaments that must have been the static discharge vanes Naomi had mentioned. As the sun moved, the large flat panes rotated and tilted, tracking it. When Jax and Naomi arrived, she looked around. "Better split up." She pointed in one direction. "You try over that way. The main control node is over there, near the center of the field."

"Who put you in charge?" Jax replied.

Naomi bowed, extending both arms in front of her. "By all means, take the lead, sir."

Jax fumed, feeling his cheeks burn. "I'll go this way." He pointed the same way Naomi had. "See if she's at the control, whatever it is." He pointed vaguely in a different direction. "You go off that way."

Naomi smirked and departed. Jax turned toward where she had indicated the control node was and took off at a jog.

A few minutes of running and Jax came around the base of a large solar array and collided with a petite red haired woman in a relief worker jumpsuit, the top knotted around her waist, her undershirt soaked with sweat. She hit the ground. "Watch out, asshole!"

Jax shook it off and extended his hand. "Sorry. You Ingrid?"

She took the offered hand and stood up. "Yeah, you the guy from that ship I saw land?" She bent down and picked up a data tablet.

Jax answered, "Yeah, and it's the ship you're about to be on, too. We gotta go."

She was about to answer when Skip cut in over Jax's earpiece, Jax held up a finger. "Boss, I'm picking up a couple of—the ridge—north." Even the *Osprey's* more powerful transmitter couldn't cut through the interference of the static discharge vanes. Jax heard only a little of what Skip had said.

Jax grabbed the small woman's arm and turned toward the camp and the waiting *Osprey.* "We gotta go."

She snatched her arm away from him. "I can walk on my own."

A solar array nearby exploded sending shards of metal and ceramic in all directions. Jax looked down at the small woman. "Then run on your own!" He shoved her ahead of him and started running.

"Captain—" Skip said, but the rest was garbled.

"Yeah, go!" Jax interrupted, ducking as another solar array exploded nearby, fire and debris rained down. Ingrid screamed.

Naomi angled in alongside the fleeing pair. "Hey, Omi!" Ingrid shouted. Naomi grinned at her friend.

For whatever reason, solar arrays stopped exploding. Only to be replaced by the whine of an approaching hovercraft. Jax stopped, motioning the two women to follow suit.

He was about to ask who they might be when a troop transport model hovercraft came into view between the thick white ceramic trunks of the solar arrays. The whine of its lift motors drowning out any conversation.

When it came to a stop a dozen meters away, several people in olive drab military uniforms jumped out and rushed toward Jax and Ingrid. Jax looked around. *Where the hell did the other one go?* One of the uniformed men shouted, "Stop right there!"

Jax finished looking around for Naomi, then said, "Uh, hey." He pointed back toward the camp. "We're just heading back to camp..."

"Shut up!" the leader of the group said, looking around. He turned to one of his subordinates. "Fan out."

Jax pushed Ingrid behind him. "Hey, look, man, we don't want anything to do with this whole civil war thing. I was hired to extract the relief camp by their company, that's it."

The man stalked toward Jax. "I'm afraid we're going to have to commandeer your craft. That Scout Ship by the camp? It will help us defeat the Imperial lackeys that have governed this world into the sorry state it's in."

"Jax, a dozen men and women are—workers. Want— them out?" Skip asked in his earpiece.

Jax shook his head. "Yeah, no."

"Excuse me?" The man had some kind of rank insignia on his shirt, but Jax had no idea what it meant. Apparently, Mariposa's rebels had chosen to break from the more traditional rank structure of the Independents and the Empire. The military man continued, "I wasn't asking for your ship. We're taking it. When we're victorious you can file for compensation."

Jax held up a hand. "I'm sorry to stop you. Your men,

the ones approaching my ship, they're about to die." He kept his hand up. "Unless you call them off, let us go, and then you can get back to your civil war. I wish you all the best."

The leader of the group poked Jax in the chest. "Look here, you miserable—"

"Wrong answer," Jax said. "Skip, Baxter, take 'em out." He didn't wait for an acknowledgement but hoped enough of his message got through the interference. He lashed out with a jab to the man's throat, which forced the man to drop his rifle. The two men and one woman who had stayed with their superior tried to bring their weapons up, but Jax shoved their leader at the woman while he leapt at the two men, so he flew sideways, taking them both to the ground underneath him. He glanced at Ingrid. "Get to my ship!" He didn't wait to see if she moved, turning back to the two men struggling under his weight. He looked at one, slugging him in the face. The other man grunted and was able to throw Jax's legs off of him. He rolled, grabbing for his sidearm. Jax was a fraction of a second too slow as he came to his feet. His eyes locked on the energy pistol aimed at him, barely a foot from his face. "Damn," he muttered.

Before Jax could choose his next words, the man opposite him flew backwards as an energy pulse struck him in the chest. The man hit the ground moaning, his chest armor smoking. Jax spun to see Ingrid holding an energy pistol. He looked over at the woman he'd thrown the officer at. She and the officer were unconscious.

Jax stood and nodded toward the two unconscious rebels. Ingrid shrugged. "They teach Krav Maga on Thursdays."

Jax shrugged. "Cool. Let's go. Where'd your friend go, the annoying one?"

"Naomi?" She looked around. "Beats me." She added, "We're not really friends or anything."

Jax looked at her. "I honestly don't care." He motioned toward the camp and the *Osprey* perched on the field beyond it, surrounded by several bodies in olive drab uniforms.

WE DIDN'T CHARGE ENOUGH

Aboard the *Osprey,* Ingrid joined her colleagues. Naomi walked up to Jax. "This ship is too small."

"Glad you found your way back." He ran a hand through his now sweaty and dust crusted hair. "You're welcome to get out and walk. I'm pretty sure you weren't on my *must retrieve* list." He looked at the ceiling, then tapped his ear. "Speaking of *must retrieve,* Rudy, have you accounted for everyone?"

"Actually, no," the droid replied. "We're missing three; someone named Thomas Chen is on the *must retrieve list...* Laura Bennet and Joel Tillum. The latter two are optional."

Jax looked around the cargo, his eyes falling on Naomi. "Where's Thomas Chen?"

She folded her arms across her chest. "Oh, you mean Thomas has to live?" Jax tilted his head but said nothing. She sighed, "Fine. He, Laura, and Joel went to the Capital two days ago. Tom thought he could negotiate for militia protection of the camp given our mission is apolitical."

Jax pointed to Ingrid, who was talking to the tall guy from earlier, Martin, and said, "Ask Ingrid how that went."

He turned and headed for the stairs. He got halfway up and turned. "Stay on this level. There's a head upstairs, but otherwise, I need you all in the hold." He pointed. "Med bay is there." He pointed to Naomi. "What's Tommie's comm ID?" She answered quickly. He moved up the stairs.

When Jax dropped into the pilot's seat, he said, "Okay, Rudy, let's see if we can't find our wayward aid workers." He gave Rudy the comm ID and said, "Once we're airborne, see if you can ping that ID, figure out where it is."

The droid said, "Will do. I've plotted a course to Darby City and the governmental building. Seems reasonable that's a good place to start. Fair warning, the capitol building, called the Palace, is in the center of the city."

Jax reached for the lift engine controls but stopped when someone said, "You can't take this ship into the city. They've got at least four or five anti-aircraft emplacements that I know of." Jax turned. It was Naomi, of course.

"And how do you know that?" he asked.

The black-haired woman shrugged. "I keep my eyes open."

Jax looked around. "So, what do you suggest?"

"There's another hovercraft in the motor pool."

Jax sighed as he stood up. "Skip, I'm taking Baxter. Deploy your self defenses."

From the speakers in the ceiling, the SI replied, "Copy."

"Baxter, meet me outside." He looked at Rudy. "Try to maintain some semblance of order, please."

"I'll do my best," the small nav droid replied, mock saluting.

Jax motioned to Naomi. "Come on."

As the hovercraft roared through the valley toward Darby City, Jax looked at his only human passenger. "Something tells me you're not just a relief worker." She ignored him, pulling her long jet-black hair into a ponytail to keep it from whipping around into her face.

While most of Mariposa might be arable, this valley and surrounding area was anything but. Scrub brush littered the valley floor, dry and brown.

From the cargo area of the hovercraft, Baxter said, "I'm picking up another vehicle, up ahead." The matte black droid stood, his feet magnetically attached to the cargo deck. Jax pushed the throttle all the way forward.

Over the whine of the overtaxed electric engine, Naomi shouted, "This seems like a reckless plan!" Jax grinned.

As they rounded a bend, another hovercraft came into view up ahead, racing towards them. From this distance, Jax couldn't tell if it was rebel or militia. In the cargo bed, Baxter raised his forearms as panels raised and barrels extended, revealing blasters. From his back, two foot-long barrels deployed, then swung around to face forward. Railguns. Jax wasn't sure if Baxter could tell who the occupants of the hovercraft were or not but didn't really care. Baxter opened fire, and less than a minute later, they sped past the burned, gory remains of the hovercraft and its occupants, what was left of them. What the combat droid's railguns lacked in range they made up for in destructive power. By the time they sped by, the railguns were stowed and Baxter's forearms looked innocuous again.

Naomi looked over her shoulder, then to Jax. "He's handy." Jax was grinning. She continued, "I'm thinking we stash this thing somewhere a few blocks from the Palace. It'll be easier to get close on foot. The last bit of news we had was that the rebels had taken the district around the government building." She hitched a thumb over her shoulder. "Especially with him. We get in, get Thomas and the others, and get back to the hovercraft. We're not the ones the rebels want, so I doubt they'll pursue, so long as we don't cause too much trouble. Getting past them, however..." She trailed off.

They rounded another bend in the trail and found themselves in the outskirts of Darby City. Small one-story cinder block and pre-fab buildings formed streets. From that close, it was obvious the fighting had taken its toll. "How long has this been going on?" Jax asked.

Naomi was looking around as they passed one burned out building after another. "About a month. There have been rebels here as long as the colony has existed, as far as I know. This particular group has been active about two months, but when the Empire pulled up stakes, the rebels made their push. The militia and the governor thought they were untouchable. Shock Troopers at the door help with that." She smiled a sad smile. "They found out the hard way that their authority was just an extension of the Empire."

"Why'd the Imps pull out?" They passed a squat building that said "Daycare" in colorful, differently shaped letters. A fire had gutted the building. "I thought this place was supposed to be the next great breadbasket world?"

Naomi pointed. "Let's park there." She pointed to a mechanic shop that looked mostly intact, except that its main service bay door had been ripped from its track. Jax followed the instruction. She finally said, "I don't know the details, but sounds like they found something in the soil near Regis. That's the city in the Southern Hemisphere. Spooked the Imperials." The whine of the hovercraft's motor faded to nothing as it settled on the stubby landing gear that deployed from its underside. "I'm guessing those rumors of the next great breadbasket were premature."

They hopped out of the vehicle, and Jax leaned out the large service bay door to look up and down the street. "Doesn't look like anyone is home."

"I'm not detecting any nearby life signs," Baxter added. His optic sensor swished back and forth.

Naomi said. "Guessing most of the civilians have fled by now, moving out of the downtown core. Too much fighting right here." She pointed down the street. "The Palace is that way." She dropped to a crouch and sprinted away.

Jax looked up at his mechanical friend. "I guess she's leading." The droid said nothing.

THREE

ONE BOT ARMY

"Damn, that's a lot of people." Jax leaned back after looking around the corner of the building they were hiding next to. The Governmental Palace was across an open park from them. Several armed hovercraft were parked in front with several dozen rebels in their olive drab getups, loitering around. All were armed. The park was littered with the burnt husks of hovercrafts and ground cars.

Naomi leaned out to look. She made a clicking sound in her throat. "Maybe they're already dead?"

"Aren't you cheery?" Jax said, then tapped his earpiece. "Rudy, you copy?"

"I'm here. How're things going? We've had a few visitors, but so far nothing Skip couldn't take care of."

"Well, there are a lot of bad guys between us and the front door. You able to get ahold of our target?"

"Yeah, he and the other two are hiding in a broom closet on the main administrative level," the droid replied. "We're pushing the power levels on the comm gear, there's a non-zero chance it'll burn out."

Jax looked at Naomi. "No such luck. Administrative floor, know it?"

She tapped her chin a few times, then said, "Yeah, I think I know a way in." She ducked back the way they'd just come, turning down an alleyway. She looked back. "Coming?"

Baxter looked down at Jax, then followed. The alley emptied out closer to the Palace by a little. Across the street was some type of shopping center, most of its windows smashed out. Smoke drifted lazily from many of them.

Naomi pointed at the building, "If we go through the shopping center, we can come out near the back of the Palace. There are a few service doors. I think we can jimmy one."

"You think?" Jax said, leaning out to look down the street toward the palace and the dozens of armed rebels. None seemed to be paying any special attention to the shopping center. An explosion on the far side of the city from them drew the rebels' attention. Several jogged off toward the explosion. He shrugged and bolted across the street. He heard Naomi's hissed expletive as he left her and Baxter in the alley. When they joined him, he tapped Baxter on the chest. "Wait here, and cause a ruckus when I give you the signal." The droid nodded and took up a position just inside the building, his forearm blasters engaging along with the two shoulder-mounted railguns.

Jax nodded to Naomi. "Lead the way."

Baxter turned and scanned the area. He crept back towards the far side of the park opposite the Governor's Palace. He took position behind an overturned refreshment stall. While he waited, he calculated the shots he'd take and in what order.

Baxter was an older model combat droid. His model had

seen extensive use during the Unification War, to offset the Independents' low number of fighters. Some said the emperor's hatred of artificial intelligence came from the losses his forces suffered at the hands of combat droids like Baxter. Baxter knew better. The man who had become the emperor was a religious zealot who had hated and lobbied against non-human intelligence for most of his career.

"Bax, ready when you are," Jax said over their short-range comms. Baxter didn't acknowledge verbally. His shoulder mounted railguns opened fire with their telltale zip-crack sound. The hovercraft to the right of the door to the Palace slid backwards from the impacts before it exploded. While those first two rounds were moving at supersonic speed, Baxter turned and loosed two more. Armored rebels vanished in red mist as hovercraft and barricades exploded.

Baxter stepped to his right as several dozen rebels took aim and opened fire on his position. Energy bolts struck him until he moved behind a statue of a man on a horse, a plasma rifle in his raised hand. His onboard diagnostics told him the damage was minimal, his armor had done its job.

As Baxter moved behind the statue, his shoulder mounted railguns let rip a dozen shots, the most he could fire in short succession before his power core needed to recharge the electromagnets in the launchers. He leaned out and raised his right arm, firing energy blasts at the encroaching rebels.

He crouched and leapt into the air, away from the crumbling statue, to land behind a burnt-out bus. As he sailed through the air, he fired both arm cannons. He consulted his railgun ammo counter. "If you could hurry up, that'd be excellent. I'm running low on slugs," he sent over the comms.

He spun out and away from the bus, his railguns barking their zip-crack staccato as supersonic rounds chewed through men, women, equipment, and the front of the Palace.

"Fall back, Bax. We'll make our way to the hovercraft," Jax answered.

Baxter fired his remaining railgun rounds, then sprinted down a street in the opposite direction of the mechanic's garage. His sensors confirmed that the few remaining were following him.

LET'S GO TO THE MALL

While Baxter was taking up position behind the refreshment stall Naomi and Jax were exiting the shopping center. The exit that Naomi had picked was across a narrow service road from the palace. A burnt out delivery truck sat a few meters away. Right where she had said it would be was a service door. She turned to Jax, "I'll go first, see if it's locked." Before he could ask her why it wouldn't be locked, she bolted, covering the distance in no time. He watched her fidget with something for a few seconds until she straightened and turned to wave him over. When he arrived she said, "Not very good locks."

He looked down at the control panel that looked pretty robust to him. She opened the door and he went in first. He tapped his earpiece. "Rudy, tell our friends we'll be there soon. They need to be ready to move."

"Copy," the droid replied, then added, "We lifted off and are hovering near the camp. It was getting a little crowded at the LZ."

"Rebels?" Jax asked.

"Them, then the Militia looking for something to tip the

scales in their favor. The upside is there was a lot of shooting and there are fewer of both sides now."

Jax nodded. "Okay, stay sharp." He looked at Naomi, who nodded. "Bax, ready when you are." The only reply was the zip-crack sound of railguns firing. He turned to Naomi. "You know your way around this place?"

She wiggled a hand. "I've only been once, but I have a good memory." She pointed ahead. "I think this should end in the main reception hall. From there, we can get to the stairs. The administrative level is two or three up."

The main reception foyer was littered with bodies: rebel and militia. The signs of a running firefight were everywhere. Chipped marble, burned wooden furniture, and more.

While it had been relatively quiet on the first level, the sound of gunfire echoed into the stairwell by the time they reached the second floor.

They skipped the second floor, exiting the stairwell on the third. More signs of firefights greeted them. They saw no sign of anyone alive. The smoke still wafting from scorch marks told them the fighting had been there semi-recently.

"If you could hurry up, that'd be excellent. I'm running low on slugs," Baxter said in Jax's ear.

Jax ran a hand through his hair. "We gotta go." He turned for the stairwell. More gun fire sounded from somewhere above.

"Fall back, Bax. We'll make our way to the hovercraft."

"Copy."

Jax turned to Naomi. "We gotta speed this up." He pushed open the door and looked over his shoulder. "Clear." They both left the stairwell. "Okay, where to?"

Naomi shrugged. "How would I know? The one time I was here, the tour didn't include the broom closets."

Jax spun in a slow circle, then stopped. "Thomas Chen!" he shouted at the top of his lungs.

"Are you crazy?" Naomi hissed.

"Thomas Chen! Get your ass out here now or we'll leave you!" Jax shouted again. He turned to Naomi. "We're in a hurry."

Two men in deep maroon uniforms rounded a corner. "Hey!" one of them, the taller one, shouted.

The shorter militia man added, "What're you doing here? Who are you?"

From behind the two militia, a heavyset man of possibly Chinese descent leaned out around a large display case of medals and trophies. "Uh, excuse me, I'm Thomas Chen."

The two militia spun. Jax raised his pistol and shot both of them in the back.

"Jesus Christ!" Naomi hissed. Thomas Chen ducked back behind the display case as the two men hit the ground.

Jax turned to her. "Relax." He held his pistol up, showing the slider set in the grip. "Stun." He turned toward the display case. "Hey, Tommy, come on!"

The man leaned back out. "Naomi?"

She waved. "Hi, Tom. Are the others with you?"

Laura and Joel came out from behind the display case. "Please help us. They've been fighting on each floor."

Jax waved them over. "Well, come on. We gotta go."

An explosion rocked the building, forcing the group to stop short of the stairwell Jax and Naomi had used.

Jax turned away from the door, smoke wafting up through the seam between the door and the frame. "Yeah, that way is probably not viable."

"Up," Naomi said. She pushed past Jax to the door and pushed it up. Smoke billowed out. She looked over her shoulder. "The roof has to have a landing pad of some sort."

"And? You said it was too dangerous to fly in," Jax protested.

"That was then—"

"There's another stairwell," the man, Joel, said. "When we were meeting with the governor, I saw him use it." He pointed down the wing the two Militia men had come. "That way."

EXFIL

Jax looked at the three terrified faces and the one stoic one. "My friend has been distracting the folks outside. When I open this door, run around the building and across to the shopping center. Don't look around. Head down, run fast." He looked around and made eye contact. "Got it?"

Naomi was trying to calm the other three. She nodded. "I'll go first. Follow me." She pushed past Jax and opened the door. She didn't stop to look back, or anywhere else, for that matter. She bolted.

Jax looked at the group. "Well? Go!" He pushed the other woman out the door, then the heavyset guy, followed by the other one...Joel, maybe? The three aid workers scrambled out the door and out of the building. They hugged the building, then darted across the narrow service road toward the waiting Naomi.

Jax looked up and down the narrow road, then dashed across. When he arrived, he said, "We go through the shopping center, then out to our transport."

For the first time since they left the broom closet, Thomas Chen spoke up. "I don't understand. You said you're here to rescue us?" He turned to Naomi. "What's happened at the camp? Who is this man?"

The probably-not-an-aid-worker looked at the man who was, in theory, her boss. "Thomas." She turned to the other two. "Laura, Joel. He's our only hope at not being imprisoned at best, executed at worst. The militia and the governor are no longer in power, and I suspect anyone that was here under an Imperial invite is no longer welcome."

Jax nodded. "We've already tangled with folks from both sides who seemed hell bent on ransacking your camp and taking anyone they found into custody." Snapping his fingers. "And they tried to steal my ship." He pointed to the section of the shopping center where he and Naomi had entered. "This way." He headed off.

Thomas leaned down to Naomi. "This went to shit fast." She chuckled and nodded.

Outside the shopping center, the results of Baxter's distraction were everywhere. Most of the armed vehicles that had been parked in front of the Palace were smoking wrecks. There were a few bodies on the ground. Far more parts of bodies were in evidence.

"I'm going to puke," Laura croaked as she stepped out of the shopping center.

"Point it that way," Jax said, pointing away from the group. He looked around. "Looks clear. Come on."

The hovercraft was right where Jax and Naomi had left it. When they entered the mechanical bay, Baxter stepped out of the shadows.

"Holy hell!" Thomas Chen shouted, then clamped a hand over his mouth, looking around to see if he'd given them away.

Baxter was damaged. He had several scorch marks on his

torso, and one of his forearm blasters had been hit. It no longer retracted completely, and was spitting sparks. His scatter light optical sensor seemed to be stuttering. The droid climbed aboard the hovercraft. "Sorry to startle you." He turned and stooped to offer his undamaged hand to the three new arrivals.

"Is this thing safe?" Joel asked as he climbed into the cargo bed.

"Until they start shooting at us," the droid replied.

"Just get in." Jax helped Laura up into the cargo bed. He turned to Thomas. "Up you go." He turned to Naomi. "Get it started." She nodded and climbed into the small cab. As he climbed into the cab next to Naomi, he tapped his earpiece. "Rudy, Skip, we're probably coming in hot. Find me an exfil location, please."

"Copy that," the *Osprey's* SI replied.

The hovercraft's motor engaged, whining as the craft lifted off the ground. "Hang on tight," Naomi said, pushing the throttle forward as the small vehicle eased out of the garage.

"Need me to drive?" Jax offered.

The black-haired woman next to him smirked. "I'm good."

"We've got company," Baxter said over the whine of the motor. Jax looked over his shoulder. Two military hovercraft were racing behind them. As he was watching, the familiar energy bolts of Baxter's forearm blaster lanced out, striking the lead hovercraft, leaving scorch marks. "My auxiliary power cells are a bit depleted."

"They're getting closer!" Laura shrieked.

"What do we do?" Joel shouted.

"Who are they? Militia?" Thomas Chen shouted.

"Does it matter?" Jax asked as weapons fire raked the

back of their vehicle, chewing up the metal tailgate. He turned to Naomi. "Maybe try to avoid their fire?"

"This isn't a fighter," the woman growled. She yanked hard on the controls, forcing the hovercraft to take a turn far too tight. They slammed into the corner of a building, losing speed.

"Okay, gimme the wheel," Jax ordered but was met with a hand shoving him away.

"I got this!" Naomi hissed as their vehicle picked up speed. The two chasing hovercraft took the corner slower but were already gaining again. The edge of town was three or four more blocks to the side of their current course, though the buildings were all single story already.

Before Jax could reply, a beam of deep purple light lanced down from the sky to spear the lead hovercraft. In the span between two seconds, the hovercraft and its occupants ceased to exist. The *Osprey* roared overhead, sending dust in every direction.

MEET YOUR HOSPITALITY STAFF

When they arrived at coordinates Rudy provided, they ditched the smoking hovercraft and walked towards a clearing as the *Osprey* roared in overhead. She circled as her landing gear unfolded, then lowered to the ground.

"Bax, get our last guests aboard!" Jax shouted as the *Osprey's* landing gear sunk into the dirt, her lift engines whining. The boarding ramp dropped and unfolded. Jax didn't wait for Naomi or the other aid workers. He ran up the ramp and took the stairs two at a time to get to the flight deck and get the *Osprey* ready to depart.

As the last of the aid workers moved up the ramp, Baxter turned his head. *Technicals Incoming,* he beamed to Skip.

"Captain, we have incoming hostiles. Three hovercraft that look like they are equipped with anti-aircraft weaponry," Skip announced.

Jax was working the controls and glanced at one of the overhead monitors. He slapped the intercom button. "Hold on. This is gonna get bumpy." From two decks below, he heard the whine of the board ramp retracting. He powered up the lift thrusters and urged the ship into the sky, just high enough that the belly mounted particle beam could be brought to bear.

The ship rocked as anti-aircraft rounds slammed into the hull. "Uh, we're not invincible. Those rounds are meant for aircraft, but a hit in the same place will puncture the hull," Skip warned.

"Then return fire," Jax said as he began to power up the main engines, pushing the *Osprey* towards the oncoming hovercraft, fast.

From somewhere deep inside the ship, a powerful whine rose, then faded. A deep purple beam of light lanced out from under the ship and carved a jagged line through the hard packed dirt, and all three hovercraft. There was barely enough of the vehicles left to explode or catch fire. Jax grinned, pushing the throttle control forward as he pulled the flight stick back towards his chair. The *Osprey* roared as she climbed higher and higher.

"We're being hailed," Rudy announced.

Before Jax could say anything, the beep from the speakers overhead announced that Rudy had accepted the comm request. "Hello? Is this the ship that just departed? I'm Governor Trellum, the legally elected governor of Mariposa. I'm asking for asylum aboard your ship!" When Jax didn't reply, the frantic man continued, "I'm in the command bunker, and my men tell me they can get me to the roof of the Palace, if you return. Hello?"

Jax looked over his shoulder at Rudy, then said to the ceiling, "Sorry, Governor. We're pretty full and already burning for orbit. I'm sure you're not a completely horrible person, and that the election wasn't at all rigged by our Imperial friends, but, well, no." He slammed his hand on a control off to the side of his station, closing the channel.

He looked at Rudy again. "Thanks, I needed to feel like a dick today." The droid made his shrugging motion. Jax glared then said. "Skip, once we're free of the gravity well, go ahead and get us going toward the ReliefCorp station."

"Will do," the ship replied, Jax's flight console going dark as the SI took over.

Jax motioned to Rudy. "Come on, you're gonna be Isaac for this little cruise." He didn't wait, heading down the stairs.

"Who's Isaac?" Rudy asked as he rolled to the stairs, sliding into the open center channel of the spiral stairwell.

The *Osprey's* lounge appeared to have been taken over by Mr. Chen and his camp management team. Jax walked to the refrigerator and grabbed a bottle of water, turning to Chen, then Naomi. "I thought you all were going to stay in the hold unless you had to use the head." He looked over to the door to the only restroom on the small ship. The door was closed. "Is this is the bathroom line?"

Chen shook his head. "It's not. We needed a place to work. It's pretty crowded down there."

Jax looked at the assorted faces, then sighed and headed for his quarters. "We'll be at your corporate station in a few days. You'll have to work out a schedule for sleeping and such." He pointed towards a bulkhead. "Only the two guest berths. Both are double bunks." Rudy had parked near the large entertainment screen. Jax pointed at the droid. "If you need anything, talk to Rudy."

FISH AND SPACESHIP GUESTS

Jax managed to avoid his passengers for most of the trip. He'd never thought much about the single bathroom on the *Osprey* until he had to fight a dozen and a half strangers for the shower every morning. Skip spent most of the trip complaining about his overtaxed resources only to have Jax tell him that they would stock up when they dropped the passengers off and that he just had to make do.

The ReliefCorp station was smaller than Kelso station, by at least half. Where Kelso was many decks above and below a large toroidal space dock, the ReliefCorp station was mushroom shaped and maybe only twenty levels tall. Docking arms reached out like spokes from the large upper section.

Jax pointed out the forward viewscreen. "Guess they wanted to be sure we knew what their mission is." He grinned as Rudy turned and followed his finger.

"Very clever," the droid replied. The ReliefCorp station was painted red with a white cross painted across the top of the mushroom cap section above each docking arm. "We've been cleared to dock at arm three," Rudy added.

"Cool. Go tell our guests to get ready to get the hell off this ship," Jax said, grinning as he thought about the payment that was about to clear his bank account.

"You're thinking about money, aren't you?" Skip asked.

"What makes you ask that?" Jax said, his smile vanishing as a blush crept up his neck.

"You were grinning like an idiot," the ship's SI replied. "You do that when you think of money. Or watch porn, but I know you're not doing the latter."

"You can shut up now," Jax said as docking arm three got closer.

The *Osprey* had two cargo access doors, one on each side of the cargo bay. Each large door had a small personnel hatch set in it. Docking arm three was a modern multimodal design, able to adjust its height and width to accommodate most ship's airlock designs, including the *Osprey*. The outer edge of the docking arm lit up as the *Osprey* got to within ten meters of it. The ship thumped once as it nestled against the docking arm, allowing it to magnetically latch onto the ship. An indicator on his console lit up green. "Good seal," Skip reported.

Jax hopped out of his seat and headed for the stairs. "Open us up, Skip."

"Roger, roger," the ship's SI replied.

"Folks!" Jax shouted as he descended the stairs into the crowded, and not very good smelling, cargo hold. "We're docked with your corporate station." The personnel hatch set in the cargo hold door popped in, then slid aside. Just inside the docking arm was Mr. Kline, the man who hired Jax.

"Welcome home, folks," the well-dressed business man said. He stepped out of the way as the tired and foul-smelling aid workers started to file out of the *Osprey*. He

61

walked over to Thomas Chen. The two shook hands and chatted a moment before the camp manager followed his group off the ship.

From the threshold, Chen said, "Thank you again, Mr. Caruso." He waved once and vanished into the docking arm.

Kline walked over to Jax. "Thank you, Mr. Caruso. We couldn't be more pleased to have our people back." Jax nodded and rested a hand on Rudy's head when the droid rolled over to the pair of humans. Kline continued, "I've authorized the rest of your payment. It should be in your account now."

Jax looked down at Rudy, who tilted up and blinked a green light on his faceplate. "It was our pleasure, Mr. Kline." He looked around the hold; loose bits of discarded clothes and various abandoned personal effects lay scattered around. "Any chance we can stock up here at your station? I'd like to top off our consumables and maybe hire a cleaning droid to come through here with a flamethrower."

The other man wrinkled his nose and nodded. "Yes, that would make sense." He motioned for Jax to follow him off the ship. "I'll help you make the arrangements."

Jax looked over his shoulder. "Rudy, you got this?"

The droid made a mechanical grumbling noise. "Sure."

"You're the best!" Jax shouted from further down the docking arm. He turned to Kline. "So, uh, Naomi Himura. What's her deal?"

The other man looked at Jax. "I don't know who that is."

PART TWO

FOUR

SPACE BULLIES

Jax lingered on the ReliefCorp station for a few hours while Rudy oversaw a crew of cleaning droids. In the cantina, some of the aid camp workers treated him to a round of drinks as thanks for rescuing them. When he staggered back to the *Osprey,* he had Skip take care of departure while he crawled into bed.

"Jax, wake up," Skip said loud enough to wake his boss but not scare the life out of him. No alarm sounded.

"What's wrong?" Jax sat straight up. He immediately reached for his trousers, lying at the end of the bed.

"I dropped us into local space to make our final course adjustment and stumbled onto a lurking Imperial patrol. They've set an intercept course, twenty minutes out. And, they're hailing us," Skip replied, his voice moving from speaker to speaker as Jax moved down the corridor past the other two crew berths, through the lounge, and up the stairs to the flight deck.

Jax finished putting on his shirt, an old *Space Rogues* shirt he picked up in a market on Ross 128b. He wasn't a fan of the movies, but he enjoyed the books his mom had given him on an old reader device. "Let's see 'em," he said, disengaging the auto-flight systems and powering up the displays set into his console. The screens blinked to life, showing an Imperial capital ship. "Great," Jax mumbled. "One of the big ones." On the screen was the wide mushroom cap forward section of an Imperial Adjudicator class cruiser. The wide forward section was almost as wide as the entire ship was long, just over a kilometer of Imperial muscle. Even at the relative distance still separating the two ships, Jax could see the heavy weapons lining the forward section in concentric rings along the stark white hull. He tapped the blinking indicator that showed the holding call. "Hi, sorry for the wait. I was asleep. This is Captain John Smith of the *Rambler*. How can I be of service?"

From the speakers a gruff voice replied, "Independent vessel *Rambler*, this is the INV-1215 *Justicar*. Prepare to come aboard for an inspection." The line didn't immediately close. Then the voice came back. "As your vessel is armed, we'll require a tactical systems lockdown beginning now until you depart." Another indicator lit up showing the waiting override of his weapons systems.

Jax tapped the button to mute the comms. "Fucking assholes." He turned to look over his shoulder at Rudy. "Ready?"

Lacking a neck that allowed for nodding, Rudy did what rock hoppers had been doing for centuries when mining asteroids in thick suits. He raised his hand and bobbed his fist up and down.

"Yes, would have worked," Jax said, smiling. He lifted his finger. "I'm afraid I'm going to have to pass."

"We will shoot you down. Prepare to come aboard—"
The channel closed.

"Oops, must have gotten disconnected," Jax said as the

massive warship slid out of view through the transparent titanium windows wrapping the front of the flight deck.

"They're charging weapons," Skip reported, then added, "Shields up, weapons hot." A warning light came on. "They've locked on."

Jax brought the *Osprey* around in a tight corkscrew as charged plasma began streaking past the ship. Several bolts of energy struck the shields, causing warning icons to light up across most of the consoles as the ship shook. The bridge lighting flickered.

"We won't last long taking direct hits, you know," Rudy quipped.

"I'm built for speed, not head-to-head combat," Skip added.

"Shut up. Both of you," Jax said as he brought the *Osprey* back on an intercept course with the much larger warship. He put the nimble Valerian Co-op infiltrator into a corkscrew. Charged plasma dashed against the shields, causing them to flare. A display showing shield strength started flashing yellow.

Jax pushed the throttle all the way forward. The Imperial ship grew quickly, its weapons batteries becoming visible. "Hold on!"

"I'm magnetically attached to the floor!" Rudy said over the roar of the engines as the *Osprey* screamed over the hull of the Imperial ship, the two vessels' shields sparking as they interacted.

The *Osprey* skimmed the much larger vessel's bow faster and closer than its guns could track, then shot over the lip of the flared forward section. Like all Adjudicator class ships, the bulk of the *Justicar's* weapons were on the wide mushroom top forward section. It had far more armor since the ship was designed to rush head on into battle, its wide forward section providing cover for smaller frigates and corvettes. The lateral gun batteries opened up, a few getting in lucky strikes against the *Osprey's* weakened shields.

In seconds, the small, far more nimble ship was past the massive cruiser. They passed the powerful engines and angled to move into the ion wash, hiding them from the bigger ship's sensors.

Jax looked over his shoulder. Rudy was using a small fire extinguisher to put out a flame under the usually unused third console on the small flight deck. "Easy," he said, turning around and making a few course adjustments before powering up the wormhole generator, causing the *Osprey* to leap into the swirling vortex of spacetime, leaving the Imperials light years behind them in minutes.

NO PLACE LIKE HOME

"The station customs official is outside the ship," Skip reported. "It's Lewis."

The *Osprey* was still ticking and pinging as it warmed up from the near absolute zero of space. Her engines were powered down and her reactor was already in standby.

The heavy external doors of the Caruso family mechanical bay were still grinding closed as the boarding ramp lowered. The static pressure barrier that kept the atmosphere from escaping the bay, sparkled just inside the track of the door. A loud clang announced the full closing of the large doors.

Jax turned to Rudy. "Let's go say hi to Lewis." He stood and headed for the stairs. "Skip, lower the ramp, please."

By the time Jax and Rudy reached the cargo hold, Lewis was walking around holding a scanning device, aiming it at the ship. When the human and droid arrived, the pudgy customs man turned. "Hey, Jax! Welcome home!" He walked over to Jax, hand extended. After the two shook hands, the customs inspector continued, holding up his scanner. "So, Mariposa, it looks like, and then..." He tapped the screen a few times. "Oh, ReliefCorp Station nine." He looked at Jax. "Anywhere else that maybe you forgot to log in your official filing?"

Jax affected a stricken look. "Lewis, my man, have I ever left things out of my customs declarations?" He put both hands on his chest, elbows out, his head tilted to the side.

The other man guffawed. "Like, almost every time you dock, Jax. It's like your thing." The other man reached into one of the many pockets of his station issued pale blue coveralls and removed a data stick, inserting it into the side of his scanning device. "Well, nothing comes up on scans, so whether you went anywhere else or not, you didn't bring anything back, so... Welcome home." The man turned to head back down to the boarding deck, then said over his shoulder, "There's a dart competition tonight at Wendy's. Just sayin'." He waved one hand over his head as the heavy personnel hatch slid open, revealing the corridor beyond.

Jax watched Lewis disappear, then turned to Rudy. "Guess I know what I'm doing tonight. You want to come with?"

The droid spun his squat cylindrical head in a full three hundred and sixty degrees. "Me? Did you just ask me to come with you?"

"You make it sound like I've never invited you to tag along before," Jax said. He turned and headed up the boarding ramp.

Rudy followed, zipping up the center of the stairwell. When Jax reached the lounge and crew berth deck, he headed for his room. "I'm gonna get changed. Skip, go ahead and power down the ship. I'll hook up the umbilical before I leave."

"Roger that. Have fun," the ship's SI replied.

Where the *Angry Spacer* was a bar tourists would avoid after being told about it, *Wendy's* was a bar they'd never be told about. Rumor had it, it was started by one of the founding families. Why it was called Wendy's no one seemed to remember anymore. No one working there was named Wendy, and as far as station records were concerned, none of the founding families had a Wendy.

Wendy's was on the lower decks of Kelso Station, near the reactor complex. The reactors made gPhones fritz out, and even the station's data network for tablets was spotty at best, usable only when one of the reactors was offline for maintenance.

"Well, if it isn't Jax Caruso!" someone shouted as Jax and Rudy entered the dive bar. The voice was a deep basso.

Rudy made a groan-like sound. "I thought they'd be gone longer." He turned. "Bye."

Marshall Delphino made his way through the crowd. He walked over. His smirk made it clear he hadn't forgotten the last time he saw Jax a few weeks ago. He was a big man, mostly muscle, and at least a head taller than Jax.

"Hey, Marshmallow, how you been?" Jax looked around the dimly lit bar. Rudy drifted over to where two other navigation droids were parked in a corner. Jax continued, "Where's your bro?"

The other man shrugged, his muscular frame causing his jumpsuit to strain in the shoulders. "Picked up a spacer chaser on Berkeley." The giant man chuckled. "I warned him, but he was in a funk and need a little boost, know what I mean? Now he's pretty much glued face down to the toilet. Been there two days now." He barked out a rough laugh and slapped a meat paw down on Jax's shoulder. "Where you been?"

Jax winced and slipped out from under the heavy hand. "Picked up a job moving folks from Mariposa to a corporate station."

"So, you have the money you owe us?" The previous joviality vanished from Marshall Delphino's face.

Jax grinned. "I heard there was a darts thing tonight. Let's talk about money after, yeah?" He moved to walk around the wall of muscle, only to have that familiar meaty paw land on his shoulder again.

"Sure, but don't forget what happened last time." The hand that was on Jax's shoulder moved to Marshall's face to lightly touch his eye.

Jax mimicked the move, touching his still a little tender eye. The black and blue had faded with the swelling, but touching it still reminded him of his last encounter with the Delphinos. He nodded and moved past the big man.

The back of the bar was just as crowded as the front except for a narrow strip between a single tall table and dart board mounted to the bulkhead. Jax approached a small woman with an inexpensive artificial eye. The cheaper stuff tended to not so much replace things as augment. Most of the hardware for her eye was mounted to her shaved scalp. The mechanical eye saw him before its organic counterpart did. She smiled. "I wasn't sure you'd be around. Big pot tonight."

Jax smiled and knelt to embrace the woman in a hug. "Laz, you know I'd never miss one of your tourneys." He stood. "What's the buy in?"

"Two grand."

"Two?! Does that come with special privileges later or something?" Jax asked, incredulous.

Laz grinned. "If you'd like, but that wouldn't even be an add on." She winked her regular eye, but something in the wiring of the artificial one made the interior illumination blink three times rapidly.

Jax did his best to hide his reaction to the come on. "What's the pot up to?"

"Forty grand."

Jax pulled his gPhone out of his pocket. "I'm in." He tapped on the icon for his banking software and sent the two thousand imperial credits to Laz. She consulted her own gPhone and nodded, walking away.

She waved a hand over her head. "We start in ten." She pointed to a board on the near bulkhead. "Lineup is there."

Rudy rolled up alongside Jax. "You gonna need me?"

Jax looked down. "Oh, now you're back? Hot date with a lady droid?"

"Something like that, idiot." The droid rolled off. Jax noticed a bright blue nav droid falling in with Rudy as he rolled away. This droid had three wheels.

"Use protection!" Jax shouted, only to receive a rude gesture from a three fingered mechanical hand as Rudy and his friend vanished into the crowd.

Jax managed to dodge the wall of human muscle called Marshall Delphino most of the night. The darts tourney went about as Jax expected. He cleaned up early on, but then realized why the lone Delphino brother was so easy to avoid.

"Christ!" Jax hissed under his breath as the massive Delphino brother walked over, both huge hands on the shoulders of Kori Lightning. "A damned ringer." Jax groaned, "Should have known better." He turned to where Laz perched on a bar stool. She winked.

Kori Lightning shrugged off the meaty paws of the larger Delphino brother and walked over to Jax. "Been a while, Caruso." She stood, one hand on her hip, the other clutching a long thin dart. Her brown eyes twinkled slightly in the flickering lights of alcohol signs.

Jax put on his best fake smile. "You, too, Lightning. Haven't seen you on Kelso in a while. You haven't been missed."

The woman smiled, turning to toss her dart, striking a perfect bullseye. "Found a pretty sweet gig on Jericho station, working security for the owner." The board lit up, and a whistle came from somewhere.

"So, what brings you back here?" Jax walked over to the table with the darts on it, picking up two. He threw each, one at a time; an inner bullseye and an outer. The board lit up again.

"Boss was visiting Earth and didn't need me, so I figured I'd come see my old friends." She turned to Marshall and blew him a kiss. "I've been talking on and off to that big lug for a few months, figured it was time to pay him a visit."

"So gross," Jax said, then added, "Let's do this." He walked over and removed the three darts from the board, handing Kori her dart and keeping his two. She grabbed her remaining darts. She looked at Jax. "This will be quick." She tossed her first dart, outer bullseye.

Jax lined up his shot. Just as he threw the dart, Kori sneezed. His dart struck just outside the bullseye in the single area. "Damn it," he hissed, spinning. She grinned, then blew him a kiss. "Bitch."

NEVER BET AGAINST THE HOUSE

"Not looking good, man!" Marshall Delphino bellowed after Kori Lightning threw her last dart. She was very much ahead in points.

Laz walked over to Jax, pulling on his arm. "Better luck next time."

Jax scowled at the diminutive woman. "You planned this, I assume? Knew that a rematch between Kori and I would draw some bets. How did I not know?"

The woman shrugged. "Gal's gotta make a living." She turned to the crowd. "Last throw!" After the cheering died down, she pulled Jax down closer. "I lucked out that you were off station until today. You got back just in time."

Jax drained his beer. "Glad I could help," he growled. He looked around, spotting one of the wait staff. "I need another!"

The server nodded and tapped something on his tablet. Less than a minute later, a droid that looked like a cross between a praying mantis and a koala bear expertly placed a new, full bottle in his hand.

"Come on, throw your dart, so you can lose!" someone shouted.

Jax looked around, couldn't tell who had said it. "Shut the hell up!" he shouted into the crowd, walking up to the throwing line.

"Better luck next time Jax-y," Marshall barked. Kori, sitting on his knee at the bar, swatted his cheek.

Jax flipped them both off. He took a deep breath, centering himself. He drew back his hand and let the dart fly. It sailed true, right to the single area. "Damn it." He hissed as the room erupted in cheers.

Thirty minutes later, Jax was sitting at the bar, having paid Marshall Delphino most of what he owed the brothers and watching the big man buy a round of drinks for everyone inside Wendy's with his winnings from the tournament.

A hand draped over his shoulder. "Cheer up. You've won plenty of these."

Jax looked over to a woman he didn't recognize and patted the barstool next to him. He motioned to the bartender. "A drink for the lady."

Jax rolled over and came face to face with the woman from the previous night. His eyes snapped open, taking in his surroundings, not his berth on the *Osprey* or even the couch in the mechanical bay office. "Hi," he said. They had spent a few hours drowning his sorrows at losing the darts tournament, before retiring for the night.

She opened her eyes slowly. "Hi." She sat up slightly holding the sheet near her throat. "I won't lie, usually at this point a guy has either snuck out as quietly as possible or is making me breakfast and coffee." She smiled.

Jax sat up, as well. "Yeah, either of those things would be less awkward than this." She nodded, turning her head slightly to look at the pile of clothes near the door to the small single room living space. His clothes.

"Do you, uh, want breakfast?" He scooted to the edge of the bed, raising the sheet to confirm his complete lack of clothing.

"Not really. I have to be to work in an hour," she said. She noticed his discomfort and turned to look at something on the wall opposite where Jax's clothes lay in a pile. Despite the previous night's activities, morning after courtesy dictated not staring.

He stood and walked over, slipping his trousers on as quickly as he could. "I'll just see myself out. Uh, thanks for last night." He looked over his shoulder. "We should do it again sometime."

She turned to look at him, smiling, just as he was buttoning up his pants. "See you around, Jax."

"Uh, yeah. You, too..." He tried to recall if she'd even said her name but couldn't for the life of him remember. The buzzing in his head made recall iffy at best. He looked pained.

"Tammy," she offered, rolling her eyes.

He pulled on his t-shirt and pressed the door control, opening the door to her quarters. After slipping out, he leaned over to put his boots on. "I was gonna say Tammy," he mumbled.

He fished the earpiece out of his jacket pocket, placing it in his ear. The smart material warmed slightly as it reformed to fit his ear canal securely. "Rudy, you read me?"

"Well, good morning, Casanova," the droid replied.

"Guessing your one-night stand woke up and kicked you out?"

Jax frowned. "It was more of a mutual—"

"Don't care," the droid interrupted. "I heard from Sandor. He has a job, possibly a big one."

Jax growled at being cut off but swallowed it, saying, "Already? We just got in yesterday. What's the gig?"

"He didn't say. Said to meet him at his office." The droid paused. "I'm on my way there now, from the bay."

"I'll meet you there. Gotta stop and get a coffee."

"She sounds like a terrible host," the droid quipped.

"Lisa...Damn it, no. Jessica..." Jax snapped his fingers twice. "Tammy was a fine host. Whatever, see you there." He tapped his ear to end the communication.

FIVE

EASY JOBS

The walk from Tammy's quarters to where Sandor lived wasn't exactly fast. The young woman who did...well, Jax had no idea what she did for a living, but it probably didn't pay all that well given that she was in what many called *The Below*. Smaller quarters, usually studios for folks that worked service industry jobs or dockside.

While Wendy's was near the absolute lowest level of the station, *The Below* was actually located just below the docks and the commercial sector. About as far from the high-class *"uppers"* as anyone could live. Sandor, on the other hand, kept his modest living space just above the docks and still well below the *uppers*. His office was above the docks, as well, but within the toroid docking facility.

He stopped at a small kiosk and got a venti black coffee. When your company wins the coffee shop wars, you get to name the drinks and sizes how you like, Jax guessed. He poured a sizable amount of sugar into it, then left, merging into the morning rush of pedestrian traffic heading to work.

Sandor must be working the night shift if he was in his office instead of work. After high school, the man had gone to trade school, then got a job in the traffic management office. He'd moved up the ranks a few times in the last few years. Jax remembered how goofy his old friend was in school, but he'd turned into quite the stable citizen now. His family weren't station founders but had been on Kelso at least a generation, his parents having arrived with the first wave of technical workers after the station spun up. His wife and son loved Jax like family. Ebo called him *kuwa jack*.

Sandor's *"office"* was really a storage closet he had hacked the station computer into forgetting about. It had a small desk, a single chair for guests, and a series of wires hanging from an open access panel. A computer terminal was spliced into a few of the data lines. Rudy had helped him set it up a bunch of years back.

Rudy was parked outside the door to the closet. His flat head turned at Jax approached. "Hi."

"He in there?" Jax said as he arrived, patting his mechanical friend on the head only to be swatted away.

"He's expecting us," Rudy said, then turned and pressed the button set next to the door. The door slid aside after a moment, and Rudy went in first.

Inside the *office* was well lit. Sandor, his brown skin glowing from the single illumination strip in the ceiling, stood and motioned his long-time friend over. "Heard you got your ass kicked at darts last night?"

Jax looked down at Rudy, who made his shrugging gesture and said, "Your failures don't need my help to spread around the station. I'm sure Sandor heard about it before you even left with Tammy."

"I think it was Jessica," Jax said, waving his mechanical friend away. He heard Rudy mumble something about *"definitely Tammy."* He turned to Sandor, taking his friend's hand. "Kori is back. She's hooked up with the bigger Delphino." He sighed and dropped into the single guest chair. "Good to see you, man."

Sandor sat down. "Good to see you, too, amigo. I heard that job you picked up went well." He turned slightly to look past Jax to Rudy. "Thought we had an arrangement aboki na?"

Rudy made his wheel sticky so he could lean sideways. He made his shrugging gesture and said, "Sorry, Sandor. That guy called the ship directly."

The brown-skinned half Hispanic, half Nigerian man waved his hand. "No big." He turned to Jax. "Glad it went well. Heard you had to give most of it to the Delphinos." He chuckled. "Guess dating one doesn't get you a discount." He grinned as Jax flushed deep red.

Jax shrugged. "Well, enough. Got the folks we were supposed to get home, home. Had to ditch an Imperial patrol on the way back here. Those assholes are getting more and more pushy out here..." He leveled a finger at his friend, "...and who I do or do not date is not up for discussion."

"That will make Tammy happy," Rudy quipped.

After stifling a laugh, Sandor nodded. "I figured that was you. A notice came in the other day about a Valerian Infiltrator that evaded a routine boarding action." He winked. "The notice found its way into the trash." He leaned forward. "So, I've got an interesting opportunity for you."

FAMILY

Sandor explained the job and the client, and when Jax didn't say "*Not interested*," arranged a meeting. The client was on station. Part of the job would entail getting him back home. Jax wasn't thrilled about more passengers, especially so soon after having to deal with the relief workers from Mariposa. Sandor confirmed it was just the one man, and it was on the way, which made Jax acquiesce. The meeting was set for the next morning, breakfast at *The View*.

As he and Rudy were waiting for a lift in the station's central shaft, his gPhone started singing. He glanced down at the screen: *Auntie*. He looked over to Rudy, holding the phone so the small droid could see the screen. The nav droid made a noise and rolled to another lift bank, pressing the up button.

Jax frowned and joined him there as he tapped his earpiece. "Auntie! How are you?"

Governor Neeti Singh didn't sound overly happy. "Jackson, what have you been up to?" The lift arrived, and he and Rudy entered. The lift started up towards the administrative levels.

Jax ran his fingers through his light brown hair. "What do you mean, Auntie? I've been off-station—"

"I know that!" she growled. Even after all the years she had spent on Kelso, her thick Indian accent from her birthplace on Earth hadn't thinned in the slightest. "I'm the governor. I know what ships are docked and which aren't."

Jax felt himself slipping back into old habits. "Yes, Auntie."

"Don't 'Yes, Auntie' me. I expect to see you in my office in ten minutes," the old Indian woman demanded. She closed the channel before Jax could reply with another "*Yes, Auntie,*" which surely would have landed him in more hot water.

He looked down at Rudy. "She's mad." The droid made a strangled sounding noise.

The lift doors slid open and Jax jogged most of the way from the lift bay to the government offices. He made it to the lobby of the governor's office with seven minutes to spare. "Hi, Geoffrey," he nodded to the admin sitting outside the double doors to the back office. "She's expecting me."

The well-dressed younger man smiled. "She is, indeed. You brought your combat armor, right?" He looked to Rudy. "Hi, Rudy. You may want to wait out here."

"That bad?" Jax asked as he pushed the announcer button next to the doors. The other man nodded once as the double doors slid apart. Jax was pretty sure he heard the man whisper, "*Godspeed.*"

"What in the name of all that's holy are you doing out there?" the diminutive Indian woman growled from behind her desk. She stood up, her bright yellow and purple sari unfolding around her as she came around her desk. "Do you think I don't know what goes outside this station?"

Jax looked around the office, studiously avoiding eye contact until, with a flash of purple and yellow, the brown-skinned woman was right in front of him, jabbing a bone thin finger into his chest. "You've been running contraband."

"Auntie, look."

She turned, hand waving dismissively. "Don't 'Auntie, look' me." She paced back to her desk and picked up a data tablet. "Do you know what this is?"

"Data tablet?" Jax offered, knowing immediately it was a bad idea when the small angry woman took a step toward him, hand raised. He raised both hands. "Auntie, calm down."

She closed her eyes and took a deep a breath. "Jackson. Your grandmother was a dear friend of mine. I watched your father grow up and loved your mother like a daughter." She turned her sad eyes on him. "This isn't what they'd want for you." She shook the tablet. "Do you think I don't get Imperial bulletins? As much as it disgusts me, this station is only independent so long as the Empire doesn't care to annex us."

Jax walked over to one of the guest chairs opposite the desk and dropped into it. "Auntie, what would you have me do? They left me an infiltrator, not a cargo ship. There's only so many types of jobs I can do. The war is over, we... they lost."

"Keep a lower profile. Like you said, the *Osprey* is an infiltrator. So, infiltrate. Don't be caught or seen." She tapped the tablet. "This one specifically calls out a Valerian Co-op Infiltrator that ran from an Imperial patrol." She raised an eyebrow.

"Fair point." He snapped his fingers. "Oh, but hey. I can't tell you specifics, but I got a gig. One that's doing good work. Legitimate work, I think." He held up a hand. "It doesn't even involve the Empire."

The small woman moved to sit behind the desk. "Oh?"

Jax nodded. "I meet with the client tomorrow. It's a good gig, helping people. I think. I don't know yet, but that's the impression I got."

She nodded slowly. "That's good." She looked him in the eye. "You know I only want the best for you, right?" Jax nodded. "Then get out of my office. I'm a busy woman."

Jax got up as she brought up a report of some type on her terminal.

MEET THE CLIENT

The View restaurant occupied the highest non-Command level of Kelso station. It was three levels below Auntie Singh's offices. Wrap around transparent steal windows provided a three-hundred-and-sixty-degree view of local space. Diners could watch ships come and go, wormholes creating light shows across the ceiling of the high-end restaurant. Depending on their table, some could stare at the neighboring nebula.

Jax walked in and nodded to the maître de. "Hi, I'm meeting someone here."

The man who looked like he'd been born a maître de raised an eyebrow. "Name?"

"Ichiko," Jax offered. Sandor had told him he'd be meeting a Nathan Ichiko, and scant little else.

The snooty host extended a hand. "This way. Mr. Ichiko commed ahead. He will be here in ten minutes." He escorted Jax to a table set for two. When Jax sat down, the well-dressed host said, "Sonia will be your server." He didn't offer more, turning to walk away.

Jax tapped his earpiece. "How's the shopping going?"

Baxter answered, "It's going. I'm down in the Market. Rudy went up to the nicer shops. I've got some engine components and other stuff from Skip's list."

Rudy chimed in, "Up top picking up groceries and other stuff."

Jax nodded, noticing someone he assumed was the potential client. "Okay, I'll check in when breakfast is over."

"Enjoy the view," Baxter said.

Jax stood as a middle-aged man of Japanese descent arrived at the table. "Mr. Ichiko?" He extended his hand.

The other man took the offered hand. "Jackson Caruso, smuggler." He released Jax's hand and motioned for the younger man to sit. "Please."

The two man sat. A woman, Sonia, Jax assumed, came over. "Good morning, gentlemen. Coffee?" Jax and Ichiko both nodded.

Once Sonia poured the coffee, took their orders, and withdrew, Jax turned his attention to the man opposite him. Round happy face, wearing a suit that Jax was certain didn't come from a vendor on Kelso station. "So, what can I do for you, Mr. Ichiko?" Jax took a sip of his coffee. He could tell it was the good stuff, not vat grown. The aroma of the brew was the best tell-tale.

Ichiko put his coffee down. "I need your help, or rather, a small group of miners I work with do. The group I represent is based on Jebediah. Small mom and pop operations, mostly. We've been the target of harassment from one of the larger mining concerns. They're trying to squeeze some of the Co-op members out of their claims. Aggressively, often violently."

Sonia returned with two plates, each loaded with bacon and eggs, both the real deal. Jax nodded to her as she departed. "I don't do security, at least not long term. Why not get the Imperials involved?" He raised an eyebrow. "And, no offense, but judging by your suit, and this meal, your Co-op can afford a lot better than me."

Ichiko sliced up some eggs, taking a bite. As he chewed, he smiled. After swallowing, he said, "We can, yes, which is why they want our claims. You probably don't want to hear this, but your reputation precedes you. And no, we don't want long-term security, especially from the Imperials. Every quarter there's a train from the stockyard to the spaceport. Unfortunately, the concern in question has been raiding our stockpiles and filling their warehouses." He paused to take a sip of coffee, then continued, "We need your help to raid the shipment. If we can take back what's ours, plus what they've collected, we'll be set up to hire a full-time security force. We also hope that a bloody nose is enough to send these bullies running." He took a sip of coffee. "It's our hope that this is still at a stage where a scalpel, you, will be more effective than a dull machete, the Empire." He pulled a tablet out of the breast pocket of his suit jacket. "This has the details, weights, sizes, dates, and such." He sliced up some more egg, taking a bite. He swallowed and added, "While you think about it, tell me about your family. My understanding is that you're one of the founders of this station?"

RECRUIT A TEAM

After breakfast, Jax stopped somewhere he was the exact opposite of enthusiastic to stop at. It had taken little thinking to decide to take the job after he scrolled through the tablet and saw the offered payment. He finished breakfast and told Ichiko he'd take the job but that he needed time to assemble a crew. The other man had agreed, and they'd set a departure time for the following evening. Jax assured him that'd be sufficient to do what he needed to do.

A moment after he pressed the announcement button next to the door, it slid open. "Well, this is a surprise," Kori Lightning said from the entry of Marshall Delphino's quarters. She'd changed her hair, the long braids replaced with two spherical afro puffs, one on each side of her head.

Jax grimaced but kept the job in mind. "I need to talk to them." He looked past Kori. "Big dummy around? Yo! Marshmallow!" He moved left and right to look past Kori and her obstructive hair. She mirrored his movements as best she could to block him.

Kori rested a hand on Jax's chest. "What do you want, Jax? Marshall and Stevie aren't here."

"I've got a job. I need Steve and Marshall for it."

Kori didn't hide her surprise. "Marshall? Steve? What for? What kind of job?' She shook her head. "I want in. I thought you hated them? I know they hate you. What makes you think they'd work with you?"

Jax shook his head. "What is this? Twenty questions? How long are you even here for? Why would I want to split the payout even more?" He tried to remember the rest of her questions. "And, yeah, we're not besties, but they're professionals, I'm a professional." He grinned. "Credits are credits."

"I'm leaving in two weeks. My boss will need me back on Jericho station then. Until then, if you're taking the Delphinos, you're taking me."

He turned slightly and exhaled. "We'll be done by then." He turned back to the ebony-skinned woman. "Come on, let's go find your new boyfriend. You and he can work out the money."

She smirked. "He's not my boyfriend, new or otherwise." She left the room and let the door slide shut behind her. "You can't still be mad about us breaking up. My understanding is that you and Stevie—"

Jax held up his index finger, then spun and stalked towards the lifts that ran up and down the center of the kilometer-long, cigar shaped station. Jax said, "Where are we heading?" He pressed the call button nearest him.

When the lift doors slipped apart, the two entered. Kori said, "Private mech bays, topside. They're visiting someone that Marshall said owed them some money." She looked away, unable to meet Jax's gaze, knowing what that meant.

Jax nodded. "Better give lover boy a call, let him know we're coming."

"Stop being a child," she replied, removing a gPhone out of her pocket.

By the time the lift stopped at the upper level of the thick donut shaped section of the station where ships docked, Marshall and Steve Delphino were waiting for them in one of the small conversation nooks that dotted the main walkways of the station. Kori walked up and planted a kiss on Marshall's cheek before sitting next to him.

Jax glanced at Steve, his face reddening slightly. "Hey." Steve said nothing.

Marshall and Kori looked at the two uncomfortable men, then at each other. Marshall cleared his throat. "Kori says you have job you want us in on? What in the name of the emperor makes you think we'd work with you?"

Jax sat down opposite them. He looked at Steve, then the couple. "Actually, just you two." He pointed to the Delphinos. "She insists on tagging along."

Kori said nothing, flipping Jax off.

Marshall leaned forward. "What's the job?" He casually placed a hand on Kori's thigh, his eyes never breaking contact with Jax's.

Before Jax could open his mouth, Kori very deliberately lifted Marshall's hand off her leg. She looked at Jax, one eyebrow quirked. "The job?"

Jax took that as his cue. "I need to boost a train car or two of raw ore. Out on Jebediah. Gotta get the schedule, the transit details, and get it done." He spread his arms. "Bigger job than me and the boys can do on our own."

Steve snorted. "The boys? Your droids, you mean?"

Jax snapped his head around. "At least they don't lie or use people."

Steve leapt to his feet. "Goddamnit, I didn't lie to you!"

He glared at Jax, then his brother and Kori. "Whatever!" He stormed toward the bank of lifts, slamming an open palm to the controls. When no lifts arrived immediately, he stomped to the wall to lean against it.

Marshall leaned over to Kori. "They have recent history."

Kori rolled her eyes. "I know that." She turned to Jax. "So why us?" She saw the look on his face. "Why them?"

Jax composed himself. "Marshall is, well..." he gestured to the heavily muscled Delphino brother, "...Marshall." He looked over to where Steve was leaning against the wall. "Stevie is an engineering whiz. We'll have to rig something up to get those cars. The *Osprey* should have the power, but she's not a cargo lifter." He paused, then said, "You, well you're smart, I'm sure we can find a use for you, so long as Marshall pays you out of his cut."

"I sometimes wonder what didn't work out with us." Kori's brown eyes looked as fierce as ever. "Today isn't one of those days."

Marshall chuckled. "Burn." He turned to Jax. "We're out. We've got a run to Shin Nihon, can't wait. Full hold of grapefruit. They spoil."

Jax pulled his gPhone out of his jacket pocket and swiped up on the screen. Marshall and Kori's devices both beeped at the same time. She had hers out first. "Holy shit."

Jax nodded. "Yeah."

Marshall snapped his fingers to get his pouting younger brother's attention. When Steve got closer, he said, "You two need to figure your shit out. I'll make the Shin Nihon run, you go with him." He pointed to Jax. "And Kori."

"Marsh—" the younger Delphino started but stopped when his much larger brother held up a hand. Steve may have been the smarter of the two, but Marshall was in charge.

Kori looked at Steve. "It'll be fun. We can share stories about his shortcomings."

Jax rubbed his face. "I have a bad feeling about this."

SIX

YOU AGAIN

It turned out that getting the Delphinos, at least one of them, onboard, was the easy part of the morning. Haggling over money and responsibility ended up taking two hours. Jax finally came to an agreement with Kori and Steve and headed back down to the lower levels. Kori had been particularly aggressive in negotiating, which seemed to tickle Marshall to no end, watching Jax squirm. For someone who wasn't explicitly needed in the first place, the ebony-skinned woman drove a hard bargain.

Jax walked into the *Angry Spacer* and walked past the bar. As he did, he waved to Lucas. "Burger?" he said as he moved to one of the booths near the back of the bar. The cybernetically enhanced bartender nodded. Jax dropped into the booth and took his gPhone out of his pocket. He tapped an icon.

"Boss?" Rudy answered.

"How's the prep going?" Jax asked as Lucas dropped off a burger and a frosty mug of beer. The burly bartender nodded and walked away.

"It's going. I ordered consumables this morning. They'll

be dropped off in another hour. Station engineering just left. The reactor is topped off."

Jax took a sip of his beer, then said, "Looks like we're down a Delphino. Any chance they'll let you adjust the food order?" He took a bite of the burger. Even though he knew it wasn't beef, he closed his eyes and let a low moan escape his lips.

"Uh, what're you doing?" his nav droid friend asked. "You better not be—"

Jax swallowed. "I'm eating lunch, you perv. Can you change the order?"

"I'll see what they say, but don't hold your breath. Oh, you had a visitor."

"Yeah?" Jax pressed. He took another bite, careful that time to conceal the moan of pleasure. Lucas had a gift for spicing up the vat meat enough you'd never know it grew on a meter-tall frame with nutrient sludge pumped into it.

"That woman from the aid camp came by."

"What aid camp? Oh, from Mariposa? Who?"

"Hmm, you know. I don't know. I know she was here, but..." The pause was a bit unsettling. "I can't seem to access that chunk of memory. I don't understand." The droid trailed off, then closed the channel. The screen on Jax's phone lit up, then returned to the home screen.

"Well, if it isn't Jackson Caruso," a woman said from behind Jax. He looked up as a vaguely familiar Asian woman slid into the booth opposite him.

"Wait, wha?" Jax stumbled over his words. The woman from the relief camp on Mariposa?

"Miss me?" the Asian woman asked, taking his mug of beer and sipping from it. Her jet-black hair was in two braids, each draped over a shoulder.

Jax regained his composure. "Not even a little." He

reached for his mug, but she was faster, moving it out of his reach. "Who are you? What're you doing here? I know you're not an aid worker, by the way. Asked your boss's boss. He had no idea who I was talking about." He extended an arm to encompass the *Spacer* and the station beyond. "And now you show up here." He munched a fry. "How'd you get here?"

She winked. "Well, you wouldn't shut up during the flight from Mariposa about your lovely Kelso station." She grinned. "Oversold, for sure." She added, "Name's Naomi Himura."

Jax took another bite of his burger and grunted. Around a mouth full of vat grown beef, he said, "We never spoke during the flight, and I don't care what your name is." He pointed at her. "What do you want?"

Naomi sighed. "I need work."

Lucas appeared before Jax could reply. "Another round, Jax?" He looked at Naomi. "Sorry, I didn't see you come in. Drink?"

She held up the rest of Jax's mug. "I'm good." She winked.

Jax nodded to the bartender, who returned the nod and departed. He turned to the Japanese-featured-not-a-relief-worker. "Plenty of work to be found on Kelso. I'm sure you'll find something to your liking." He took the last bite of his burger. "I'd put in a good word for you, but well, I don't know you from Eve." Before she could reply, he continued, "I'm serious. We never spoke during the trip out from Mariposa. You leave a tracker on my ship?"

"How gauche, no." She grinned. "Once I was on the ReliefCorp station it wasn't hard to hack into—what did you call him—my boss's boss, Kline's, terminal and back track where he'd been and who he'd paid."

Lucas returned with Jax's beer. He reached for the empty plate. Naomi slid it out of his reach, eyeing the untouched fries. Lucas smiled. "I'll bring ketchup." He strode towards the small kitchen area at the back of the space.

Jax took a sip of his beer. "Who are you?"

"Naomi Himura, I already told you." she replied.

"Not an alias?" She shook her head. "Okay, and what do you want? Why do you think I'd have a job for you?"

Lucas swung by the table, leaving a bottle of honest-to-God ketchup. Jax looked at the bottle, then Naomi. "He never gives me real ketchup."

"I'm cuter." She turned the bottle over, and as she thumped her palm on the bottom to dislodge the thick crimson condiment, she said, "You seem like you have your shit together. I figured after your performance on Mariposa, you'd probably have something lined up." She popped a ketchup covered fry in her mouth. "Plus, I hacked the station network. You're pretty popular here." She sCo-oped up more fries. "Your family are founders, posh."

Jax waved his hand again. "What about Kelso station says *posh* to you?" He downed the rest of his beer and stood. "Bye."

CROWDED SHIP

When his alarm went off, Jax rolled over to slap the screen of his gPhone, and through sleep crusted eyes, spotted someone sitting in the chair that he would have sworn was covered in discarded clothes.

"Wha..." he groaned, rolling back over to sit up and rub his eyes. He blinked the sleep away and was face to face with Naomi Himura, the woman who was most definitely not an aid worker, but very possibly was a cat-burglar.

"Hi," she said. She was leaning back in the chair, the picture of relaxation in a forest green jumpsuit. *How long has she been sitting there?* he wondered. He slipped his hand under the pillow for the stunner he kept there. "You have thirty seconds to explain yourself." He withdrew his hand, stunner activated. He leveled it at her casually, a light on the top of the device indicating that it was charged.

She held up both hands. "I know this is a bit unorthodox, but—"

"But nothing. You hacked ReliefCorp to find out who I was, then followed me here, then broke into my quarters while I was sleeping."

"I was there for all of that. You don't need to recap it for me." The green eyed woman—*her eyes are freakishly green*, Jax realized—said. She sat up straight in the chair. "Like I said, I was impressed with what I saw on Mariposa. I think we could make a good team. I've been reading up on you. I know you've got some type of job on Jebidiah, something about—"

Jax shot her.

"Mr. Ichiko, I'd like you to meet Kori Lightning and Steve Delphino," Jax said as the pair arrived at the mechanical bay that housed the *Osprey*.

The well-dressed man bowed. "A pleasure to meet you all." He turned to Jax. "I am ready when you are, Captain."

Jax held his hand out to the lowered boarding ramp. "Rudy will show you to your berth." He turned to the other two. "Come on. I'll show you to your berths. Sorry, space is limited, you'll have to share." He turned and walked up the ramp, not seeing the look Steve and Kori exchanged. "Skip, get the pre-flight started, please."

Kori whistled as she exited the stairwell onto the common deck. "You haven't changed a thing." She walked over to the sofa, running a finger along the top. The old cracked leather moved under her ebony fingered touch. She looked over at Jax, smiling. "Hi, Skip," she said, tilting her head toward the ceiling.

"Kori! It's good to see you again," the ship replied.

Steve looked around. "Kind of a dump." An offended sounding noise came from the ceiling speakers.

Jax grimaced and turned toward the short passage to the crew and guest berths. "This way."

The hatch to the berth Jax had assigned to Kori and Steve swung open, "Here you go." When the two entered, Jax didn't bother to hide his grin when they turned to look at him. "Sorry, infiltrators aren't enormous." He winked. "I'm sure you'll figure something out." He turned and grabbed the hatch handle. Over his shoulder he said, "We take off in ten." He closed the hatch behind him.

He knocked on the door next to Steve and Kori's. "Mr. Ichiko, we take off in ten." A muffled reply came through the door. He tapped his earpiece. "Baxter, you all set?"

"Roger that. Everything is secure." Jax nodded as he reached the staircase.

Ten minutes later, Jax was sitting at his station staring out the wrap around window at the mechanical bay beyond. The heavy doors were open, and yellow strobing lights flashed in the bay.

Rudy was in his station. "We're cleared for departure." When Jax didn't reply, the droid pressed, "You okay, boss?" When Jax still said nothing, the droid rolled over to stop behind the pilot's seat. A metal hand reached out and rested on Jax's shoulder. "Boss?"

"Huh? Sorry." Jax looked over his shoulder at his small mechanical friend. The rust red paint that covered most of the droid's body was chipped in places, highlighting the droid's age. "We ready?"

The droid tilted forward on his smart material roller ball, the best he could manage a bow. "Yup, all set." As the droid rolled backward towards his station, he asked, "Gonna be okay having Steve aboard?" He moved a metal hand in a motion to take in the rest of the ship. "And, you know."

Jax waved the droid's concerns aside. "It is what it is, I guess. Flings happen. They rarely turn into more." When the droid didn't press on the other issue, Jax reached for the intercom button. "Everyone should sit down. We're about to depart."

Outside the transparent steel windows of the flight deck, a heavy freighter passed by the open mech bay. The five-kilometer-long monster of a ship lumbered past, likely heading for a parking spot a few kilometers from the station where dock workers in cargo mover suits would ferry the cargo modules into the main space dock. "Big one," Jax said to no one in particular. The moment the aft section of the massive hauler passed the open bay doors, he worked the flight controls to raise the *Osprey* up off her landing gear and eased the throttle forward. The sub-light engines powered up, pushing the nimble infiltrator out of the bay. Several thuds echoed through the ship as the landing gear retracted and locked down, hull panels sliding into place over the gear. On a small display off to the side of his console, Jax saw the mech bay doors sliding closed.

"Sending you our exit vector," Rudy announced a moment before one of the screens on Jax's console came to life, showing him their assigned route away from Kelso station.

Jax eased the *Osprey* away from the station and around another lumbering heavy freighter that was inbound. He looked over his shoulder. "Wormhole generator?"

"Charged and ready," Rudy reported.

Jax nodded. "Next stop, Themura." He activated the wormhole generator and watched as a rip in the fabric of space time opened and the *Osprey* leapt through.

"You shot me, you fucking prick," Naomi growled from the chair they had tied her to in the engineering space aboard the *Osprey*.

Baxter was standing next to her. "She has a colorful vocabulary."

The angry woman looked up at the combat droid. "Fuck off." She turned back to Jax, her face scrunched in anger. "You shot me. You didn't have to shoot me."

Jax tilted his head. "Well, you seem to have no concept of boundaries, don't seem to take no for an answer, and somehow knew a lot more about this job than you should." He leaned against the reactor control panel. "Mind explaining?"

"I gotta pee," his prisoner retorted.

"Then you'd better talk fast." He grinned. "Long way to Themura, and you're not getting up until I get answers."

"Fine. Untie me, gimme a tablet or your gPhone."

Jax nodded to Baxter, who extended a wicked-looking blade from under his forearm. One quick motion freed Jax's unwelcome guest from the chair. Baxter stood back, the blade sliding back into his arm.

Jax reached over and picked a data tablet up off the workbench next to the console. He tossed it to Naomi.

The moment she caught it, the screen lit up. He seemed to recall that happening on Mariposa, too. As she held the device, Jax could see data scrolling across the screen, the regular user interface gone. Naomi coughed, and that was when Jax noticed glowing blue lines running up her arm. Slowly more and more blue lines were tracing up her other arm, along her neck, up to her cheeks. A line traced around her left eye. The blue lines pulsed. Occasionally one would fade and another pulse brightly.

She looked up from the tablet in her hands. Each finger had a blue line running its length, ending at her fingertip. "Ever hear of the interface program?" She tossed the tablet back to Jax. By the time he caught it, the screen had the familiar user interface, no visible sign of what had just happened.

"Never heard of it," Jax admitted.

"It was an Imperial—" she started.

Jax stood bolt upright, interrupting her. "Imperial?"

She held up both hands to stop whatever he was going to say. The blue glow had faded completely from them. "I'm not an Imperial. At all. Fuck those guys." She grinned, but it was in no way a happy expression. "Toward the end of the war, the emperor wanted to create something to counter the Independent's use of intel-droids." She looked up at Baxter. "Those things could infiltrate any system they came near." The matte black combat droid didn't move.

She held out her right hand, turning it over, the blue glow seeming to turn on and off at will. "So, he created interfaces."

Jax leaned forward. "So...you're a cyborg?" He reached out to poke her forearm. She batted his hand away.

Her face crinkled. "No. Not that there's anything wrong with 'borgs, but no. It's more tightly coupled than that." She shifted in her seat, clearly not comfortable with the topic. "Interfaces needed to be able to pass for," she gritted her teeth, "human. One hundred percent un-modded human." The blue tattoo like patterns on her face lit up. "Biological circuitry, organic storage media." She pointed to the base of her skull, then her midsection.

"Cool," Baxter said, breaking his ominous silence.

Jax looked at his mechanical friend, then turned to Naomi. "Okay, so you're some type of Imperial science project. Why are you here?"

She inhaled. "The war ended before the emperor deployed us. Once he had his empire, he had no use for us. He terminated the project." She looked around. "I really do have to pee."

Jax sighed. "Fine, come on." He turned to leave Engineering. He stopped and looked over his shoulder. "When they ask, you stowed away." He didn't wait for her response.

TIGHT QUARTERS

When Jax came up the stairs, he found Mr. Ichiko and Kori sitting at the small table near the kitchenette looking over a tablet while Steve was watching what looked like an episode of *Star Trek: The New Adventures*. Not one of the better episodes, Jax noticed. "Oh good, you're all here." He made a *come on* motion. "This is...uh, my...er, girlfriend. Naomi."

"Your—" Kori started.

"Girlfriend?" Naomi finished, then coughed. "Girl-friend, yeah. Hi. We met a few weeks ago, one of those hookup apps." She looked around the room pantomiming swiping on the screen of her phone. "Couldn't get enough of him after that." She nudged him on the side, then spread her hands apart while grinning at Kori. Jax groaned as he closed his eyes and pointed toward the forward bulkhead and the hatch leading to the head. Then he studiously examined something on the ceiling.

When the hatch closed behind Naomi, Steve paused the vid. "Girlfriend? Couple weeks? Wouldn't that be around when..." His face had a red hue, but Jax wasn't sure if it was an angry or embarrassed blush. Probably the former.

Jax ran a hand through his hair. "Uh, yeah. Anyway, she'll make herself useful and won't get in the way." He made sure to not make eye contact with Steve.

Ichiko nodded. "Mr. Caruso, this is highly irregular." He was trying his best to keep his scowl under control. "I hired you and a crew of your choosing. Now you are adding in a..." He seemed to be testing the word out. "...Girlfriend?"

Jax tried his best to mask the grimace he was sure he was wearing with something blander. "I understand, Mr. Ichiko. It wasn't my intent to surprise you. I assure you, Naomi understands the need for discretion." He glanced at Kori, who was clearly not buying what he was selling. He looked back at his client, who seemed to be thinking it over.

Ichiko inhaled. "Very well. That will have to be good enough for me," the elder man replied, turning his attention back to the data tablet between him and Kori. He looked at the ebony-skinned woman. "Your turn."

Kori stared at Jax for another few heartbeats before turning her attention back to whatever game she was playing with Mr. Ichiko.

Naomi walked out of the head and took in the room. Jax nodded to her, then tilted his head towards the corridor where the berths were. "Come on... honey." The last word was clipped, and he blushed a deep red the moment it left his mouth. She followed him toward his quarters.

From the common deck, Kori shouted, "Dinner in an hour, lovebirds."

Jax groaned and opened the door to his quarters. When Naomi crossed the threshold, she turned. "I will not be sleeping with you." When his mouth opened, she raised a finger. "Ever."

"I...no, that's—" he stammered.

Her face was set in stone. "Ever." She looked around the room, at the single unmade bed. She reached down, picking up a pair of boxer shorts from the edge of the bed, letting them drop to the ground. "Ever," she repeated.

"I had to come up with something." He held his arms out wide. "What would you have had me say? Hey, everyone, this is the weird chick that can hack computers just by touching them and learned too much about our job to leave behind, because who the hell knows if she's trustworthy?"

"I mean, that's quite a mouthful. 'This is my friend Naomi' probably would have sufficed."

Jax exhaled loudly. "Yeah, no. Our client is paying us to rob someone. That someone is a criminal organization. While noble, still not legal. I didn't want to risk him scrubbing the job, or at least scrubbing the paying me part."

Naomi sighed and mumbled something in what might have been Japanese, Jax wasn't sure. "Fine, but like I said, no." She pointed to the bed. "You can sleep somewhere else."

Jax rubbed his face. "I'll sleep on the floor."

"Jax?" Skip interrupted.

Jax looked at the ceiling. "What's up?" He glanced at Naomi, who had an eyebrow raised. "Sorry. Skip, Naomi. Naomi, Skip."

"Pleasure," the SI replied tersely. "Jax, we've got company."

"Who?"

"Imperials," Skip and Naomi said at the same time. Jax looked at her like she'd grown an extra head, then turned his attention back to the ceiling speaker. "How?"

"They must have been loitering just outside detection range of the station. We're thirty minutes from Kelso, and they just dropped out of a wormhole twenty thousand klicks ahead."

"They've been nosing around Kelso more and more," Jax explained to no one in particular, though Naomi assumed it was for her benefit. He exhaled. "Okay, stay in contact and follow their instructions. I'll get everyone ready." He opened the hatch and looked over his shoulder. "Well, come on, girlfriend." He held up a finger. "They won't be able to detect your glowy thing, will they?"

She scowled and pushed past him, much more forcefully than he expected a woman of five-four to be able to. "No, they won't."

SEVEN

MEET THE IMPERIALS

Jax came down the stairs from the flight deck to see his guest and temporary crew all lounging in the common space. Kori, Naomi, and Mr. Ichiko were crammed together on the sofa with Steve occupying the lone chair.

Rudy dropped down the central column and rolled out of the staircase.

Jax took in the scene. "Cozy?"

Mr. Ichiko looked over. "Captain, your collection of video entertainment is truly phenomenal. You are a connoisseur. So many pre-Empire classics."

In Jax's earpiece, Skip said, "I hid the porn."

Jax smiled and nodded, knowing the camera pick up in the common room would see him. He said to the others, "Thanks. We spend a fair bit of time in the black, so it helps to have quality and quantity in entertainments."

He walked to the small kitchenette and opened the refrigerator. "Beer?" Yeses all around.

He returned to the lounge section and distributed the beers. He grabbed one of the chairs belonging to the small dining table and pulled up next to the chair with Steve sitting in it. The two exchanged a look, then tried to not look like they exchanged a look. Jax looked at Kori, who grinned and wiggled her eyebrows. She made a motion toward Naomi that Jax ignored. "So what're you all watching?"

Naomi gestured to the screen. "Something called *Fringe*. They appear to be a secretive governmental agency that solves mysteries."

Ichiko added, "With the help of what appears to be an insane man."

Jax smiled. "It was a good show, you know, for two hundred odd years ago. It didn't make the cut when the emperor, then senator, started his purity nonsense." He turned to look Steve. "Wouldn't have pegged you for a fan of old-timey vids."

Steve looked at Jax. "Plenty you don't know about me." Before Jax could respond, he added, "Our client picked it."

Ichiko shrugged. "The oldies are the goodies. I think that's how the saying goes." He grinned. "I never approved of then-Senator Stenson's politics. Such a closed-minded man." He spread his hands. "And here we are."

Everyone nodded solemnly. Jax extended his hand toward the large bulkhead mounted screen. "By all means."

The episode of *Fringe* started playing.

***

Three days later, Skip woke Jax up two hours earlier than he should have. "Jax, get up!" the speaker in the ceiling blared.

Jax sat bolt upright. "What? What's wrong?" The lights in his quarters raised to daylight levels.

"What's going on?" Naomi groaned from the bed.

"Imperial patrol. Burning hard to intercept," Skip answered.

"Same tub as the last time?"

"What's going on?" Naomi repeated.

"Negative. IFF reads the INV-1203 *Resolute*. Another Adjudicator class." Skip answered, still ignoring the woman.

"Strong name," Jax said, slipping his pants on and grabbing a *Fantastic 7* tee shirt off the chair in the room's corner. He reached for the hatch handle.

"Should I wake the others?" the ship's SI asked.

"What the hell is going on!" Naomi shouted, getting out of Jax's bed.

He turned to her. "Were you not listening? Imperial patrol." He opened the door and left his quarters. He walked past the berth next to his, where Mr. Ichiko was bunking, and kept walking. He neared the door to the berth he'd given to both Steve Delphino and Kori. He banged a fist on the door. He heard a series of shouts and groans and grinned. "Yeah, go ahead and gently wake our client," he said as he reached the staircase.

Naomi stepped out of Jax's quarters, slipping a sneaker on. She looked at his bare feet.

Rudy popped up from the deck below. Jax stopped on the staircase. "What were you up to?"

The droid continued up toward the flight deck. "I was taking a nap."

Jax reached the flight deck and immediately saw a blinking red indicator. He sat down and tapped the control. "This is Jeb Bartlet, Captain of the *Joey Lucas*. How can I help you?"

A nasal voice replied, "You can power down your engines and prepare to be boarded."

Jax affected his most innocent sounding voice. "Oh, is there something wrong, *Resolute*?"

"Transmitting your docking vector now. Auto flight will take over at five thousand kilometers, you'll surrender weapons control then. *Resolute* out."

The massive shape of the sideways mushroom cap of the Imperial ship was visible now to the naked eye, the massive name stenciled in ten-meter-tall letters, *RESOLUTE*.

Naomi, Steve, Ichiko, and Kori crowded out of the staircase. The Japanese man asked, "What's going on? Your ship said the Imperials were harassing us?" He looked past Jax at the now even larger *Resolute*. "Oh, I see." The man looked around. "I don't think I need to tell you all that our mission should not be shared with the Imperials." Everyone nodded. "Also, if we can arrange it, it'd be better if they didn't see me."

Jax raised an eyebrow. "Why is that?"

"Long story. One I'm happy to tell when we're safely on our way away from that Imperial monstrosity."

ROUTINE STOPS

The *INV-1203 Resolute* drifted past the *Osprey*, the smaller ship dwarfed by the massive cruiser. Jax and the others were down in the cargo hold while Skip handled flight ops until the Imperial vessel took over flight control to bring the *Osprey* in. The docking vector provided took them passed the massive mushroom cap forward section and to a small hanger on the main body of the ship.

"This doesn't look very comfortable," Mr. Ichiko complained as he lowered himself down the ladder into the small weapons module on the underside of the infiltrator. While Valerian Co-op Infiltrators had several weapons types at their disposal, the underbelly-mounted particle beam cannon was their most powerful. The particle beam weapon system was self-contained in the lower section of the ship, under the cargo bay. It was not much more than a crawlspace, but thanks to the exotic matter conditioner and other highly energetic components, there wasn't a sensor around that would pick out a single bio-sign in that area of the ship.

Jax shrugged. "That, or chat with the Imperials." The

older man descended the ladder. He looked up. "See you soon. Be safe." He waved as the rungs folded flat against the wall and a hatch slipped over the access way. Jax turned to Rudy and Baxter. "They'll scan you two, then expect you to hang around the ship, so depending on how long this takes, you may need to slip him some food or water."

The matte black combat droid turned his mostly featureless face toward Jax and the others. "We got this, boss. He'll be fine." His optic receptor had a red scatter light that swished side to side.

Naomi asked, "Where did you get a combat droid, anyway?"

"His parents," Kori offered before Jax could answer. He turned and glared at her. "What? Was it a secret?"

Jax was about to answer when Skip announced, "Entering the *Resolute's* bay now. Touchdown in five, four, three, two, one." The *Osprey* lurched slightly as she came to a rest on the deck of one of the *Resolute's* landing bays.

"Let's meet our friends." He moved to stand more in the center of the hold. He turned to the others. "Remember the cover story." Everyone nodded, though Steve didn't look happy about the agreed upon story.

Several clunks and whirs announced the lowering of the boarding ramp. Baxter moved to stand in the hold's corner. The sound of heavy boots boarding the ship echoed. It didn't take more than a few seconds for the first Imperial shock trooper to come up the spiral staircase and stand in the hold facing Jax and the others. Three more troops emerged from the stairs to be followed by the ship's sub-commander. She was in her mid-forties, her crimson colored uniform stiff enough that it likely stood on its own when she went to bed at night.

The woman walked up to Jax, looking him up and down

before saying, "You're the captain of this ship?" She glanced at Baxter, raising an eyebrow, but said nothing. Imperials looked down on droids and the humans who associated with them.

Jax nodded. "That's me, Jeb Bartlet." He tried his best to plaster his most winning smile on his face. "How can we be of service to the Empire?"

The woman tutted, "You can stay out of the way while my scanner crew goes over your ship. Where are you headed?"

Kori coughed. "Uh, we were headed for York." She pointed at Steve and Naomi, "It's their honeymoon." Jax nodded. The two tried their best to look equal parts innocent and in love with each other. Steve looked slightly more uncomfortable than Naomi.

The sub-commander walked over to the two fake newlyweds, eyeing each of them in turn. She turned to Kori. "And you are?"

Kori reached for Jax's hand. "I'm his girlfriend." She pointed to Baxter, then Rudy. "We do odd jobs when in port. The droids help."

Jax smiled. "Sub-Commander..."

"Pettit," the woman offered.

Jax nodded. "Sub-Commander Pettit, have we done anything wrong?"

She motioned to two of her shock troops. "Escort them off the ship."

"Sub-commander?" Jax said, his voice higher, more urgent.

Pettit spun to face Jax. "You've done nothing wrong, that we know of, Captain Bartlet. If you comply, this will take very little time, and you can be on your way." She motioned to her troops. She looked over at Baxter. "Do we need to worry about that thing?"

Jax replied, "No, he's inactive right now." He looked at Rudy, who had been sitting near the staircase doing his best to be unnoticed. "Stay out of their way, be helpful." The droid made a series of random beeps and whistles in response.

THE BRIGHT LIGHT OF CIVILIZATION

The crew of the *Osprey* was shown to a small lounge area off the docking bay where they could wait for the search of the *Osprey* to be completed.

Jax walked over to a window where he could see the *Osprey* and a few other craft, all Imperial. "Hate these assholes," he growled.

Kori grunted. "The long arm of civilization keeps getting longer." She looked around, squinting. "They've been getting harder and harder to avoid."

Steve nodded. "Yeah, we had to dump cargo three weeks ago out near Valhalla. They seem to perch at wormhole transfers all over the Outer Edge these days." He shook his head. "Bastards cost us on that one. That's why Marshall had to stick to the job we booked."

Jax turned. "Wait, wasn't that...?"

Steve looked at him straight faced. "Like I said, I wasn't lying." He turned and stalked to a vending machine set in the room's corner. "Any of you have Imperial credits on you?" Naomi reached into a pocket on her jumpsuit and walked over.

"Cap?" Rudy said over Jax's earpiece.

Jax looked around, then walked over to where Steve and Naomi were examining the vending machine. Catching Kori's eye, he nodded toward the machine and brushed his ear. She nodded, then turned and joined them at the machine. She nudged Naomi, nodding toward Jax as both of them moved to stand between Jax and where they were pretty sure a camera was mounted. "What's up?" he asked in a whisper, turning to make sure it looked like he was looking at a selection of fried vegetable snacks next to Steve. While their comms were low-powered, meant for close range, and heavily encrypted, it was still risky to talk for too long. Especially inside an Imperial ship.

"I'm worried they'll find the vault," the droid replied.

Jax tapped his chin. "See if you can distract them, but if they do, they do. There's nothing in there right now that would cause too big a problem." He reached up to tap his ear, then paused. "Don't forget to feed the cat." He tapped his earpiece. He looked at Naomi and Kori, nodding. He looked to Steve next to him. "Split a bag of pickle wrinkles?"

Naomi nudged Kori. "What was that all about?"

"You'll have to ask your... boyfriend." She winked.

Rudy did his best to silently follow the scanning team as they wandered around the *Osprey*. The sub-commander had left the ship shortly after Jax and the others. The scanner crew dutifully ignored Rudy while he tried to *accidentally* get in their way, beeping and whistling his apologies.

The upside of being a droid, even an older model, was that he could hold a conversation over encrypted comms while still moving through the ship politely harassing the team of Imperials.

"Hey, droid!" someone shouted.

Rudy spun his head in a full circle, beeping politely.

"Come up here!" the voice said, this time from the deck above, the sound passing through the open spiral staircase.

Skip, can you come up with something to keep them from the vault? Rudy sent over the ship's wireless network.

I will do what I can, the ship's SI replied.

Rudy rolled towards the stairs. He beeped and whistled, hoping that the shock troops got, *"Excuse me, coming through. Please get out of my way,"* out of the sounds. When one of the scanner techs ignored him, he reached up and pinched the man on the butt. With a yelp of surprise, the road block removed itself. When he reached the common deck, he looked around.

"Over here!" a woman shouted. She waved to him from the end of the hallway that led to the berths. "One of these is locked."

Rudy followed over, and the scanner tech pointed to the door to Mr. Ichiko's assigned berth. He made a series of beeps and whistles: *How odd. Please wait a moment.* He added a few bonk sounds for emphasis.

"Open, it. Now," the woman insisted.

Rudy made a show of fumbling for pockets his body didn't possess before reaching up to the announcer pad. Knowing that Skip was watching, he pressed the button, then pushed the hatch open. He spun his head to look at the woman. When she said nothing, he beeped, *You are welcome.*

From below, the sounds of shouting echoed up. Rudy turned for the stairs but was shoved aside as the woman he'd just helped pushed him out of the way. By the time he got back down to the hold it was obvious what the commotion was. Fire suppression foam was all over place.

Skip said, *Sorry, I'm not good at distractions on short notice. I made it seem like the guy in the armory tripped something then shot foam everywhere.*

Rudy watched two scanner techs leave the armory, wiping foam off their uniforms.

I think it worked, though, Rudy replied.

WHO'S CLEANING THIS UP?

"Fucking Imperial dickheads!" Jax fumed as he flung his hand hard enough to dislodge fire suppression foam from his hand to splat against the bulkhead.

Steve walked over to the access hatch leading to the particle beam cannon equipment crawlspace.

Jax walked to the staircase. "I'll get us underway." He pointed to the armory hatch. "Guess what you all are doing?" He didn't wait to hear their replies, heading up to the common deck as quickly as he could.

As he dropped into the pilot's console, he asked, "Skip, we ready?"

The Imperials found nothing that would have given them cause to keep Jax and the others in custody—much to Sub-Commander Pettit's displeasure, from what Jax could tell. When her scanner team, as far as they knew, accidentally caused the fire suppression system to activate, she ordered the search cut short.

"Yup, they're insisting on auto flight out to five thousand, but we're cleared to go. I got the sense they were eager to see us leave."

Jax powered up the grav-lift motors, lifting the *Osprey* off its landing gear. With the expected clunks, the gear retracted into the ship. Jax spun the ship around to face the large hangar doors. He looked down at the blinking indicator and sighed as he pressed the control. The flight controls slid away from him as the ship left the docking bay under the control of an Imperial flight controller somewhere in the massive warship. Watching the controls make adjustments, Jax growled, "I hate auto flight."

"Try being me," Skip replied. "Someone is controlling my physical body from a distance. It is disconcerting."

A few minutes later, the flight controls moved back into position, nearly knocking Jax over. He tapped the intercom button. "We're flying free. Wormhole in five."

On the small display showing the rear camera view, he watched as the Imperial ship receded. He knew the ship would track them as long as they were sensor range. The type of ship the *Osprey* was, how many were aboard her, her transponder ID, and likely a lot more metadata would be logged and sent back to New Terra to be logged in a massive database.

"Wormhole in one minute," Jax announced on the ship-wide intercom. He looked over his shoulder. "Everything dialed in?"

Rudy made his nodding gesture, metal fist bobbing up and down at the wrist twice.

A countdown on Jax's console reached five. "Four, three, two, one," he said, then pushed a blinking blue button. Outside the cockpit, a vortex of blue and green swirling gases spiraled open. Lightning like electrical discharge danced around the event horizon. The *Osprey* leaped into the vortex, and in a blink, the swirling energy collapsed, leaving no trace that anything had been there.

The interior of the wormhole was a twisting tunnel of the same blue and green energy. The flight controls retracted from Jax's pilot seat into the console. He turned. "How long?"

Rudy wheeled away from his console. "Two days." He paused, then added, "Three course changes along the way."

Jax went down to the commons deck to see everyone sitting around the lounge. "Done with the de-foaming?" he asked, grinning.

"If I never see fire suppression foam again, it'll be too soon," Naomi groaned, reaching up to wipe a glob from her hair.

Jax headed for the kitchenette. "We've got two days to kill. Who's hungry?"

Kori nudged Steve in the ribs. She coughed and said, "Stevie makes a killer lasagna, if you've got the ingredients." The younger Delphino brother glared at his sibling's love interest, who smiled and made a *go on* motion.

From the kitchenette, Jax said, "Uh, yeah, I think we do, actually. I'm game..." He paused, trying to compose himself. "...If you are?" When Steve nodded, Jax extended a hand toward the various cupboards.

Steve got up and moved over to the kitchen area to help Jax. Mr. Ichiko looked at Naomi and Kori, eyebrow raised.

Kori chuckled and glanced at Naomi. "Rumor is they hooked up a few weeks ago. Stevie won't tell me anything, but I know they got in a fight and Stevie decked Jax before he and his brother shipped out on their last job."

The other man leaned back, exhaling. "I see! I had wondered what the tension was about." He shook his head. "Young people, so wasteful of time." He smiled. "I guess I am the only one on this ship to have not slept with our captain." He turned in his seat to watch the two twentysomethings prepare dinner for the others, missing Naomi's pantomimed choking gesture. He turned back to the other two. "Well, maybe they'll figure it out while we're in wormhole transit." He pointed to the screen. "More *Fringe*?"

The next morning, Jax eased out of his quarters as quietly as he could so as not to wake Naomi.

"Hey, Skip," he whispered, looking at the ceiling as he padded into the common deck lounge.

"Yeah, boss?"

"What's on the to-do list?" He pressed a few buttons on the coffeemaker and smiled warmly as the familiar clunks and whistles sounded, announcing that the brewing process had started. Even though it wasn't real coffee, it did the job and smelled good.

"The biological system needs some love. Our trip to Mariposa, and now all of you, are doing a number on it."

The coffee maker dinged. Jax pulled a mug from the cupboard. "Anything less, you know...gross?"

There was a pause as the ship's SI scanned the substantial list of things that needed doing. "Lots, but depending on how long this job lasts, you really should look into the biologicals." Another pause. "Sorry."

Jax sipped his coffee. "Wonder if I can make Naomi do

it?" He shook his head. "I guess it's my responsibility." He moved to the staircase.

In the quarters that Steve and Kori were sharing, Skip said, "You're clear. He's down in Engineering."

"Thank God," Steve said, standing. "He was gonna try to get us to clean the shit tank, wasn't he?"

"He actually debated making Naomi do it," the SI replied, then realized his slip up. "I'm sure he was joking. Girlfriend and all. You know, the sex."

Kori ran a hand down her face. "Thanks, Skip, that'll do." She looked at Steve. "Coffee and an ass-kicking?"

Steve grinned as he opened the hatch. "Mario Kart 2099?"

She nodded. "You know it!"

The biological systems for the Valerian Co-op Infiltrator were tucked in along the port and starboard sides of the ship, accessed from the engineering space. With space at a premium, especially on smaller craft like the *Osprey*, the biological systems were tightly integrated and operated at high levels of efficiency.

Jax removed a gloved hand from an access panel and examined it. "We need a bot for this."

"That's pretty offensive," Baxter said from the opposite side of Engineering, where his charging cradle was situated.

Jax held up the gloved hand. "This is shit, shit from four people, not to mention the way too many we rescued from Mariposa." He made a face as he peeled the glove off so that it was wrong side out. He dropped it into a recycler and grabbed a fresh pair. Before slipping both on, he sipped his coffee. "Gimme some work music at least."

Skip obliged by playing some *oldies* from the overhead speakers in the relatively large engineering area. Jax reached into the access panel again, this time with both hands. Somewhere inside that particular piece of equipment was a high-powered impeller meant to churn the tank, pulverizing any chunks. When the tank reached a certain fill level, the slurry was sucked down into another chamber where it was exposed to vacuum in order to form it into a frozen cube. Said cube would then be jettisoned.

Jax dry heaved while holding his head back away from the opening, looking up and away from his work. "So gross."

Mr. Ichiko was the last to rise. He found Steve and Kori still on the sofa engaged in the cartoonish race of their lives. Naomi was sitting at the small cafe table reading something from a data tablet, a cup of coffee steaming next to her.

"Good morning, my friends," the jovial Japanese man said as he moved to the coffeemaker.

Naomi looked up. "Good morning." She smiled.

"Hey," Steve and Kori said in unison, their eyes never leaving the main display and the game on it.

"Where is our captain this morning?"

Steve snickered, and Skip answered, "The captain is down in Engineering making repairs to the biological systems."

The older man made a face, scrunching his forehead. "Oh, that doesn't sound fun."

"Possibly the worst job on a ship," Steve said as he leaned to the right as his cart, driven by a mushroom man, drifted off the course slightly. "Damn it!"

"Ha!" Kori shouted as her cart, driven by a woman in a pink dress, roared past.

Hours later, Jax walked up the staircase. "You all need to get more fiber."

Steve looked at him. "Man, you need to shower, now."

"You reek," Kori agreed.

Mr. Ichiko nodded. "You do indeed stink, Captain." He held up a pot, steam wafting off it. "I am preparing lunch. It will be ready when you are showered."

EIGHT

WELCOME TO THEMURA

The *Osprey* settled on its landing gear in the Apophis City spaceport two days later. City was a generous term as far as Jax was concerned, not that he'd seen a lot of cities, but well, this one was underwhelming. As the boarding ramp lowered, unfolding to touch the duracrete, Jax walked down, Rudy behind him.

A black ground car with dark windows and no identification was waiting at the edge of the landing pad they'd been assigned. Mr. Ichiko descended the ramp. "That's my ride." He turned and offered his hand to Jax. "I look forward to hearing from you when your errand is completed."

Jax looked around. "Nice ride. I never did ask, why Themura? If your Co-op partners are all on Jebidiah?"

The other man nodded once. "Ah, yes." He made a motion taking in Apophis City beyond the ring wall of the spaceport. A few mostly gray towers could be seen. "Recruiting. There are a dozen or so private security firms here in Apophis, a few more in Jenkins Township. I'll hitch a ride to Jebidiah from here once I hear from you."

Jax shook the man's hand. "We'll be in touch." The

other man walked to the car. A door opened and the older man got inside, glancing back at Jax and the others briefly before the door closed and the vehicle departed.

As Ichiko's car drove away, a heavy ground truck pulled up. A work crew jumped out. The team lead waved. "We'll get you topped up and ready to go."

Jax nodded. "Can you flush and recharge the biologicals? I had to do some in-situ work, and well, it's not my specialty."

The dark-skinned man nodded. "Sure thing, bub. Will take a few hours."

A colleague added. "At least."

Jax looked at the group. "Grab a drink while this fine man and his people work? Maybe there's a dartboard somewhere?" He grinned. He turned to the ship. "Skip, go ahead and button up. Baxter, you're on duty."

"The *Empty Keg* got a dartboard," the work team lead said as Jax and the others started off toward the pedestrian exit of the spaceport. Jax nodded his thanks.

The *Empty Keg* was two blocks from the spaceport. "And I thought the *Angry Spacer* was a shit hole," Steve said as they entered.

"I've never been to Themura," Kori mused as they made their way to a booth. "What do they do here?" She reached into her pocket and removed her gPhone to look it up.

When they sat, Rudy said, "I'm going to explore. Call if you need me." He didn't wait for an answer, rolling off toward the far side of the moderately sized bar. Jax could see at least one droid of unknown age in the corner. It turned at Rudy's approach. It was the first droid Jax had seen since arriving. They were getting fewer and fewer as the emperor's hatred of them permeated the empire.

A tall, thin man, a greasy apron over what looked like similarly greasy trousers and t-shirt, ambled over to them. "May I take your order?" He was at least two-and-a-half meters tall. Probably from one of the asteroid mining settlements, initially. Even with bone and muscle augmenting meds, he must have been in agony all the time.

Jax opened his mouth, but Naomi spoke first. "You got New Terra Lager?" The man nodded. "Four of those and four shots of tequila." He looked down at his tablet, then back up. "Food?"

This time Kori spoke. "Basket of fries and a basket of wings." The server nodded again and left. She placed her gPhone on the table. "So, according to WikiGalaxia, Themura is mostly prairie. There's only one ocean, freshwater. It covers almost fifty-five percent of the planet's surface." She wrinkled her nose. "Apparently full of eels, which are one of the main sources of protein. This colony officially sucks." She turned to look toward the doorway the droid had exited through. "You don't think the wings are—?"

"Eels?" Jax offered. "Probably."

They chatted about nothing in particular for a few minutes before the server returned with their drinks. "Please, enjoy. Your food will be here momentarily."

Kori watched the man leave. "He's more pleasant than I expected." The others nodded.

Naomi grabbed the shot glass in front of her, motioning to the others to follow suit. She held the drink. "To making a lot of money." Everyone echoed her toast and downed the shots. Jax looked at the woman, her light brown skin glowing under the dim lighting, one eyebrow raised.

Jax tapped his empty shot glass on the table to get Kori's attention. When she looked up, he tilted his head. In the opposite corner of the bar from them, two men had just started playing darts. The two excused themselves as Rudy rolled back to the table. Naomi and Steve eyed the droid before the younger Delphino finally said, "So what's your deal, Rudy?"

The droid's matte red head turned to focus its camera pick up on Steve. The lens spun a few times, focusing. "I was born to a poor coal mining family back on Earth in West Virginia. Pa worked the mines. Ma made a little here and there doing laundry and other household work." When Steve stared blankly at the droid, it said, "What do you think my story is? I've been with the Caruso family since before Jax was born. His parents bought me new, upgraded my systems, and I've been the family navigator ever since. When they were killed, I was on the *Osprey*. Skip and I barely escaped. When we got back, I became Jax's navigator." The lanky server ambled back over with a tray of food. Rudy rolled out of the way, mumbling, "Goober," as he did.

The server looked down at the droid, his expression one of mild indifference. He deposited the food. "Refills on your drinks?"

Steve nodded, not taking his eyes off the dart game. "Yeah, another round." The man departed.

WE ALL HAVE A TYPE

After the server left, Steve turned to Naomi. "So. You and Jackson? Couple weeks now?"

Naomi shifted in her seat. "Uh, well." She met the other man's eyes. Rudy's optical sensor whirred as it spun, focusing on her. Jax had been hesitant to give her any more details than necessary regarding his relationship with Steve. Even though they'd been together a few days aboard the *Osprey,* she could see that he was still feeling something for Jax. "No..." When both of Steve's eyebrows shot up, she held up a hand. "It's complicated, but that was for the sake of the client. It worried Jax that Mr. Ichiko would cancel the gig if I just showed up."

Steve took a breath. She could see a great deal of tension drain from his face. It was replaced with suspicion faster than Naomi thought it should be. "So, what's the deal, then? Who are you? What're you doing on this job?"

She looked over Steve's shoulder to where the dart game was still going on across the bar. It looked like Jax and Kori were winning. The ebony-skinned woman was doing her best to downplay her skills to encourage bets. "I needed work. I think I'd be an asset to Jax."

"I didn't see you come aboard?"

"Oh, he stunned me and brought me aboard before everyone else met up, had me tied up in Engineering," Naomi replied.

The server arrived with their drinks, stopping Steve's reply before it started. As he cleared the empties from the table, Steve couldn't wait. "He stunned you and tied you up in Engineering?"

The server stopped moving, then realized he'd stopped and immediately grabbed the last empty glass, straightening back up. Naomi smiled. "Don't worry, it's just a kink of his, totally consensual." She winked at the server as he flushed and backed away, his long legs taking him away from the table quickly. Steve's mouth was hanging open. She asked. "Can you not do that?"

"What?" he asked, regaining his composure.

She picked up her drink. "Sit there mouth open like a dying fish, and two, loudly say shit like 'he tied me up.'" She took a sip. "He had a good reason to stun me, if I'm being honest. I broke into his quarters." She grinned, remembering his sleep addled brain trying to cope when he woke up to her sitting next to the bed. "Anyway, it's all good now." She looked across the room to Jax. "I think."

"So, you're not sleeping with him?" Steve probed.

"God, no," Naomi said. "He's not my type."

"Your type?" Steve repeated. She could see even more tension ease off him, now that he realized that she hadn't stolen Jax, and wasn't sleeping with him.

"Don't get me wrong, dad bods are fine." She looked over Steve's shoulder again at the two other members of their little crew. "But I like my men a little leaner," she grinned, "and gingery."

Steve nodded, lost in thought as he ran a hand through his dark brown hair. Naomi watched him for a minute until she was sure he would not continue the conversation. She withdrew her gPhone and opened a game she played to pass the time.

Rudy had been silently watching the entire exchange and finally said, "I've been nagging him to lay off the junk food for a while now."

Naomi set her gPhone down as Steve's eyes refocused. They both looked at each other and laughed.

"What? He's not exercising enough and drinks too much beer." The droid's head turned from person to person at the table. "Don't get me started on his unhealthy obsession with Cheez Dingbats."

Between deep breaths, Steve said, "Dad bod." While Naomi, in an imitation of Rudy, said, "Cheez Dingbats."

After a solid minute of laughter, Naomi looked at the man opposite her, getting serious. "We're cool?"

Steve nodded, taking a wing from the basket. "We're cool." He bit into the breaded and texturized eel meat. "Sorry for the cold shoulder on the way here. He's not great at making things up on the fly. The timing lined up with when we started ... hanging out." He finished his wing, adding, "I don't know what's gonna happen, but the notion he was seeing others made me, I dunno, equal parts angry and embarrassed."

Naomi smiled. "All good, man. I hope whatever you two have going on, works out."

Steve grunted. "Thanks. Who knows? My brother hates him. Like, hopes he dies, hates him."

"Awkward," Naomi observed.

"And you?" Rudy pressed, tilting forward on his roller-ball. He knew all about the Delphino/Caruso feud. Jax and the two brothers had carried on an antagonistic relationship since they were in primary school together. Mostly it had been the occasional fight or prank or some other childish— in Rudy's opinion— thing.

"Well, I don't hate him." Steve smirked, turning to look over to where Jax and Kori were very obviously running the table with the locals.

MAKING NEW FRIENDS

Jax and Kori came back to the table to get their new beers and snatch handfuls of fries. Jax tried an eel wing, Kori refused. Steve had eaten most of them. Naomi asked, "How'd the hustle go?"

"That obvious?" Kori asked, her brown eyes twinkling as she slid a small pile of physical currency into the middle of the table. Naomi whistled.

Jax watched Steve eat another of the misleadingly named *wings*. "How are you still eating those?"

Steve shrugged. "I dunno. They're not bad as long as you don't think about what they are. I mean, they're basically a boneless wing."

"Made of eel," Naomi reminded.

"Well, yeah, but we have wings on Kelso. Have you ever seen a chicken?" Steve raised an eyebrow and looked at Kori and Jax.

Rudy chimed in, "There are no chickens on Kelso, nor are they frequently imported." His head spun a full rotation and he added. "Very expensive to transport."

"Well, shit." Jax exhaled. "Thanks for ruining wings,

forever." The younger Delphino brother made a rolling motion with his free hand and bowed his head. He popped the eel nugget in to his mouth.

Kori looked over to where they'd been throwing darts. "We should probably pay up and get out of here."

Naomi tilted her head. "Why? What's wrong?"

Steve, the smarter Delphino by far, replied, "I don't think your marks were as dumb as you thought." A small clutch of men and women, still near the dartboard, were exchanging glances with each other and cold stares toward Jax and the others.

Jax made a face. "Sore losers." Several of the men started toward their booth. He looked at Rudy, "Can you get us paid out?" The droid made its nodding motion, then rolled off toward the bar. As the nav droid passed another booth, it swiped a steak knife off the table.

"You cheated us," one of the men said when he reached their table. He was big, bigger than any of Jax's friends. He was wearing stained overalls and reeked of fish, and his red hair was slicked back against his scalp. He must have worked in the eel business. Apophis City stretched all the way to the ocean two kilometers distant. Another man joined him as Jax and the others all stood to leave.

The second man grabbed Jax by the shoulder. The new arrival was wiry and bald. He had a very lovingly manicured mustache and goatee.

"Get your goddamned hands off me!" Jax shouted, reaching up and wrenching the man's thumb, driving him to his knees, a yelp of pain escaping out from under the mustache.

As more people from the other side of the bar joined in, the first man reached for Jax only to have his hand stopped by Steve. "We're leaving now." He said as sternly as he could muster. His brother was the muscle of their operation, normally.

"You cheated me," the first man growled. "I want my money back!" he shouted, spit flying from his mouth.

"No," Jax said through gritted teeth as he released the other man and wiped spit from his face. The first guy had at least ten inches on Jax. "We didn't. You're just not very good at darts."

Before anyone could say or do anything further, Naomi sailed through the air to land on the back of the large local. She was a blur of blue jumpsuit and jet-black hair, raining blows down on her surprised target. Steve used the confusion to leap onto the man Jax had brought to his knees. Jax and Kori turned to punch a big woman who was attempting to flank them. She had two broken beer bottles in her hands. She fell with a thud, out cold.

In seconds, fists, furniture, and glassware were flying around the bar. Apparently, the locals liked a good fight, regardless of the cause. The lanky server was shouting for everyone to calm down, but he was largely ignored.

Jax fell and rolled in time to avoid a kick from what looked and smelled like another eel rancher. He got to his feet in time to see Steve throw a very angry woman off his back and into the big man that Jax had been squaring off against earlier.

From somewhere near the bar, people started screaming and shouting. The angry mob began shifting away from something. The fighting near Jax and the others paused as the wave of confusion passed through. Then without warning the last of the angry locals parted and a blurry red tornado came into view. Rudy, a knife clutched in each little metal hand, was rolling towards them. His head remained stationary relative to his rapidly spinning barrel-shaped torso. Blood flew in wide arcs any time anyone made the mistake of getting too close. "Well? What're you waiting for?" the droid said as he shifted his course towards the front door of the *Empty Keg*. As he reached the door, Rudy stopped twirling and moved to let his human crew mates rush out the door. He had intended to start spinning again, but several large men grabbed him and carried him back toward the bar.

"Rudy!" Jax shouted but was pushed out the door by Kori and Steve.

The group burst out of the *Empty Keg* onto the street. Jax and Naomi were the first out, Steve and Kori right on their heels. Kori waved. "Come on!" She started jogging in the general direction of the spaceport.

Right on their heels, the first of the bar patrons started to exit the building, weapons drawn. Jax didn't hesitate. He drew his blaster, shooting the first two people to exit the building, in the legs. Steve pulled his own blaster and fired into the shoulder of a woman who emerged with a snub-nosed blaster rifle in one hand. She screamed and fell to the ground, dropping her weapon.

The man whom Jax and Kori had hustled came out, a blaster pistol in each hand. "You don't come into the *Keg* and hustle us and expect to get away with it!" He leveled both guns at Jax. Before he could fire, he screamed and fell backward, revealing Rudy and his steak knives.

As Rudy rolled passed the man, he said, "I hope you know a good reconstructive surgeon." The man moaned, blood seeping from the backs of his knees.

Jax and Steve exchanged a look, then turned and ran down the street, the former tapping his earpiece. "Skip, we're gonna need to leave, in a hurry. Baxter, we're on our way." Naomi, Kori in tow, sprinted past him.

CHASED OUT OF TOWN

"There's the ship!" Kori shouted as they ran around the bow of an old freighter. Blaster bolts struck the ship, raining sparks. Jax glanced up, thinking the owner would not be happy to have more damage to what looked like a ship held together with good thoughts and insta-epoxy. The trip from the bar to the spaceport had been a sort of running gun battle. After losing a few more of their crowd to minor wounds, the locals had fallen back, but when they entered the spaceport, their anger and boldness returned. It helped that they seemed to have called ahead for reinforcements. Jax and the others had barely gotten through the pedestrian entry before the mob got to the tunnel in the ring wall.

Kori turned back and fired several blasts from her pistol. Someone screamed.

The *Osprey* was at least two hundred meters away, over open landing pad. Another freighter, only slightly bigger than the *Osprey,* lifted off, blowing dirt and dust around the landing area. Everyone had to slow down and shield their faces. The freighter they were hiding behind was the only cover.

Jax looked at the ship. "Baxter?"

A dark blur leapt from the top of the freighter to land with a thud two meters from the approaching crowd. A booming voice said, "I will cut you all down. Stop right where you are." The matte black droid had both forearm blasters deployed, having fixed the damaged one, and one of his shoulder railguns was tracking independently. "It will be gross."

A scraggly fellow in worn coveralls stepped forward, aiming his blaster pistol at the combat droid between him and the crew of the *Osprey*. He fell to the ground, a burnt hole between his eyes. Smoke wafted from the barrel of the blaster mounted in Baxter's right forearm. He had raised his arm faster than anyone could have possibly processed.

"I do not have a stun setting. Anyone else feeling bold?" Baxter asked. He looked over his shoulder, red scatter light optical sensor swishing side to side. "Go, now." The group left the safety of the freighter, now with more blaster scarring than it had landed with, and sprinted to the *Osprey*.

"Captain, I'm picking up chatter from the local authorities. They don't seem to know what's going on but are en route to the spaceport," Skip announced over Jax's earpiece. From behind, he heard an occasional blaster shot and scream of pain. Baxter must be having fun. Skip continued, "They're rolling heavy, too."

"Move it! Cops inbound!" Jax shouted, trying to increase his pace. "Heavily armed!" As soon as everyone was under the wing of the *Osprey,* Jax called out, "Baxter, time to go!" The boarding ramp dropped, unfolding as it did. Jax ushered the two women up before going up the ramp himself, leaving Steve to cover them. The younger Delphino had his weapons drawn and was standing on the edge of the ramp.

Steve was watching the combat droid when out of the corner of his eye he spotted a now familiar rust red object. "You're starting to make me rethink my ideas on droids," he said as Rudy rolled up, his knives nowhere to be seen.

"I'm chock-full of surprises," the droid replied, rolling up the ramp past Steve.

Jax dashed as fast as possible to the flight deck, taking stairs two at a time. The controls were already awake and ready when Jax dropped into his seat, panting and sweating. "All set, Skip?" he wheezed.

The flight controls slid out of their standby position as the ship's SI replied, "You bet." The rumble of the engines began to build.

A blaster bolt ricocheted off the transparent view screen, causing Jax to flinch. He looked out the window to the crowd standing around the ship, many taking pot shots with their pistols. None of their weapon's fire would hurt the *Osprey*. Jax shouted, "Hold on down there!" assuming Skip would route his voice through the shipwide intercom. He put his hand on the grav-lift controls. With his free hand, he flipped the angry mob off, then pushed the lift controls forward, causing the *Osprey* to surge straight up off the tarmac. The thruster wash sent several of the nearest and lightest weight members of the mob rolling backwards away from the infiltrator as she rose. As the ship cleared the ring wall that made up the perimeter of the spaceport, Jax spotted a dozen or more hover cars with red and blue flashing lights on them. They were racing toward the vehicle entrance to the port. Behind them were two heavy personnel transports.

Rudy said, "That was fun." He popped up the center of the stairwell and moved to his station.

Jax glanced over his shoulder as he powered up the

main sub-light engines to boost them out of the atmosphere. "Thought I'd have to buy another droid." Rudy made a weird sound. Jax added, "We need to talk about you and those knives." He raised an eyebrow. "What did you do with them?"

"I left them on the tarmac," the nav droid replied nonchalantly. "Didn't need them anymore, and there are plenty of knives aboard the *Osprey*."

"Okay, that's...well, that's disturbing." Jax turned to focus on flying as the *Osprey* gained altitude, her engines screaming until the atmosphere thinned. He ignored the flashing light on the communications panel.

A few minutes of flying in silence towards the edge of Themura's gravity well and Jax mused out loud, "Think that little incident was a big deal?"

Rudy said, "Well, we shot up a bar and a bunch of locals. Yes, I think that *little incident* was probably a big deal. Oh, by the way, Imperial frigate coming over the horizon."

Skip chimed in. "He's right, a notice was just posted on the planetary network." The SI paused as if he was reading over the notice: "The Independent trader *Penelope* is wanted for disorderly conduct and discharge of a firearm in public. I'd say we should put Themura on our *Don't visit too soon* list. They don't have our real ident, so that's a plus." The SI paused. "Oh, and that frigate is hailing us."

Jax shrugged. "Ignore them. Five minutes to wormhole." He then added, "I mean, I don't know what the big deal was. That reaction, and the determination they showed, really seemed a bit much. Chasing us all the way into the spaceport?"

Rudy tutted, "You hustled some locals. What did you think would happen? Worse, these particular locals seemed both itching for a fight, and out to have each other's backs." The droid paused. "Maybe that bodes well for Mr. Ichiko and his hiring of security forces from this planet. They seem to like to fight."

Jax nodded his agreement, then said, "Ideally, they're not supposed to know they've been hustled until we're gone." Rudy made a rude sounding noise. He turned back to the flight controls. "Wormhole in two." He looked at the ceiling. "Skip, you got this?"

"Course plotted, wormhole generator online and ready," the SI confirmed.

Jax stood and walked to the staircase.

PART THREE

NINE

RELATIONSHIP STATUS

The *Osprey* made it to safe wormhole distance long before the Imperial frigate got close enough for a detailed scan, let alone close enough to lock a tractor beam. To be safe, Jax dropped into local space a few times, changing course slightly. It was unlikely the Imperial ship would try to track them, but it paid to be safe. At least Jax thought so, sometimes.

Once the excitement of being chased off Themura and avoiding an Imperial ship died down, Naomi told Jax about her conversation with Steve. Jax hadn't been thrilled, but it did make things a little easier aboard ship. The night before they arrived in orbit over Jebidiah, Jax and Naomi came clean over dinner, or at least partially clean. They had agreed to keep her special skills under wraps a little longer, especially the running from the Empire part.

Being able to evict the living computer interface from his berth was the highlight of the trip, as far as Jax was concerned. He missed his bed and his privacy. Kori and Naomi had agreed to share a room, allowing Steve some space of his own. Jax wasn't sure the two women sharing a room was a good idea, but it was better than him having an uninvited guest in his quarters.

Both Jebidiah and Themura were in the outer territories of the Empire. Themura was a bit more established, having been started nearly fifty years prior, long before the Unification War and rise of the empire, by mostly colonists from the North American continent on Earth.

Jebidiah was a new colony, all things considered, only about twenty years old. The Empire founded the colony after the war when a survey ship detected the delibdomin deposits from orbit. It was their first colony lottery. It was also the last, so far.

Ever since, it had been a bit of a gold rush on the damp rocky planet with families, small and large businesses, and everyone in between rushing to the planet to strike it rich. The lottery winners had been given a head start, but it wasn't much.

The system's twin stars made wormhole travel iffy at best, forcing ships to leave their wormholes in the outer system and make their approaches at sub-light. It took a day of sub-light travel to reach orbit.

The *Osprey* was orbiting the planet while Skip built as accurate a model as he could of the surface, in particular the spaceport, the train line, and the ore depot and surrounding towns. Much of the population of the planet resided in the foothills of the mountain range that had been found to be full of delibdomin.

"Our first order of business is to get down to Abda and get a lay of the land. Ichiko gave me the name of a stockyard foreman to find and schmooze for details, said he was sympathetic to the small operators." He took a breath. "We do know that the train is set to leave," he consulted his gPhone, "in two days."

"That doesn't give us a lot of time," Steve said. He craned his neck towards the spiral staircase leading down to the cargo hold. "I'll need most of the time to rig something up. I've been searching the internex for specs but wouldn't mind getting specifics of what's in use down there. Lot of makes and models out there for ore cars."

Jax nodded "That's your and Kori's main job once we touch down. Naomi and I will scout the town and find our mark."

Kori pursed her lips. "Why you two?" She looked at Naomi with a knowing look that Jax didn't understand.

"Because—" Naomi started but stopped when Jax held up a hand.

"Because," he said, "I'm in charge." He pointed to Steve and Kori. "I need you two to get the rig built. Steve, you're our resident techie. Kori, well, you wanted to come along, so help Steve." He pointed to Naomi, "She's got different skills."

Steve and Kori exchanged a look, then looked at Naomi, who just smiled innocently. The knowing looks were weirding Jax out. He was going to have to talk to Naomi on the way to town. Everyone had been acting weird since Themura. A thought occurred to him. "Plus, depending on where our stockyard foreman falls, the two of us have a better chance at flirting our way into what we need to know."

Naomi cleared her throat. "I know you didn't just suggest pimping me out for information." Her look made it clear where she fell on that idea. Kori's face made her thoughts on it obvious, as well.

Jax held up both hands, opening his mouth to explain but was cut off. Skip said, "I think we're all set, boss. We can land whenever you're ready. The local space control folks in

Salma are friendly enough, but curious why we're loitering in orbit. They've asked if we needed help with anything a few times."

Jax nodded. "They bought our ident and cover story?"

"Hook, line, and sinker," the SI replied.

Jax smiled. "Be right there. Get into position for landing in Abda."

"Copy," the SI replied.

Jax looked at the others. "We're going, the moment we set down. Get your shopping lists ready. Time isn't on our side." He turned and headed up the stairs.

"Different skills, huh?" Kori asked. Steve was taking a sip of water and almost spat it everywhere. Instead, he had to double over from the coughing fit he was experiencing.

Naomi looked Kori in the eye. "We all have things we're good at." She winked.

Up on the flight deck, the flight controls slid into position as Jax sat down. He flipped a few switches and several of the monitors nearby came to life. Rudy, from his station, said, "I've got the plot. It's on your screen."

Jax nodded. "Got it. What're we looking at? I know the spaceport is in Salma, so..."

Rudy made his throat clearing noise. "Yeah, 'spaceport' isn't quite the term I'd use, even for Salma, and not at all for Abda. We'll be landing in a field, a muddy one at that."

"Are there non-muddy ones?" Jax asked.

"No."

"Oh, goody," Jax muttered. The *Osprey* shuddered as she struck the upper atmosphere of the colony world. Plasma streamers began forming along the leading edge of the deflector shields.

JEBIDIAH

The boarding ramp dropped and made a sort of plop noise as it settled, then sunk an inch or two into the gray mud of their landing pad. From the ramp, Jax looked around. "Well, this is disgusting." He looked around, seeing the *Osprey*'s landing gear settling into the muck.

From behind him, Kori said, "I'm not stepping in that."

From behind her, Naomi added, "Me, either."

"These are the only boots I brought," Steve offered.

Rudy appeared at the top of the ramp. "A ground vehicle should be here shortly. I booked it to take you two into town." He tossed Naomi a data tablet. "That's got everything Mr. Ichiko provided on it." She caught the device and nodded.

A few minutes later, what could only be described as a motorized cargo vehicle with oversized knobby tires rolled up. It was automated, the onboard RI capable of driving the thing and nothing more. Rudimentary Intelligences, or RIs, had no personality or feelings of any type. They were not self-aware. The cart moved as close as it could to the boarding ramp, but Jax still had to jump from the ramp to the vehicle. Naomi made the jump a bit more gracefully than Jax. As she dropped into the seat opposite him, she reached forward and slammed her open palm on the cab. "Let's go." The vehicle beeped twice and accelerated away from the *Osprey,* kicking up a rooster tail of mud that clung to the underside of the infiltrator. Kori shied away from the spray, moving back up into the ship and pushing Steve ahead of her.

The town of Abda, according to the WikiGalaxia entry Jax had looked at aboard the *Osprey,* had a population of about fifteen thousand people, nearly all miners or in mining adjacent fields. From what he could put together, plus what little Ichiko had shared, Abda was mostly small Co-op efforts, plus a handful of large mining concerns. The Co-op Ichiko represented was one of the mid-sized efforts. The town further up the line was mostly the larger mining conglomerates.

The ground car came to a halt. The driver RI beeped three times, then four times. Jax looked at Naomi. "Do you know what it wants?"

She shrugged. "Why would I? I don't speak droid."

He looked at her, then raised both hands and wiggled his fingers. "You know, your computer talk mojo thing." She sighed.

Before she could try to interface with the ground car's RI, Rudy said, "It's saying *you're there.*" Through his earpiece. Jax looked around, "Really?" The ground car repeated its beeps. "Okay, okay, fine." He climbed out of the vehicle. Naomi followed. Thankfully the actual roadway was paved and mostly free of glop.

As the ground vehicle trundled away, Jax approached a grease-covered man in worn overalls. "Excuse me, we're looking for someone. Adamic, Tommy Adamic. He's a foreman at the depot."

The burly miner looked Jax, then Naomi, up and down. "If he's the foreman of the depot, then I guess he'd be at the depot, don't you think?" He smirked and pushed Jax aside, continuing on to where ever he had been going.

Jax frowned. "Rude." He raised his voice. "And the depot would be where?"

From fifty feet away, the miner held an arm up, his hand pointed to the north.

Naomi followed the gesture, then retrieved her gPhone from her jacket pocket. "Let's go. We can scope out the depot, then see if our soon-to-be friend Adamic has a bar he likes. Guessing the workday here ends in about two hours." She held up her gPhone so Jax could see the clock. He nodded.

The depot was on the outer edge of town, where the train line ran past on its way to Salma and the spaceport there. "There's mud everywhere." Jax complained, tapping his boot against a perimeter fence post. The depot sprawled nearly a kilometer of storage barns and stockyards. Men in power loaders wandered the grounds, moving immense crates of ore from barn to staging area in preparation of the train's arrival in a few days. Each crate and barn was labeled with the Co-op or company the ore belonged to.

Naomi watched. "So..." she trailed off, lost in thought for a moment, watching the activity below. She pointed to a storage unit being carried by two power loaders. "Those must be the cargo modules that they load onto the train. Big." She turned and put a finger over Jax's mouth to stop the joke he was about to tell. "Can the *Osprey* lift one of those?" The modules were indeed quite big. It looked like each train car must hold two modules. The tops of the modules looked like they hinged open, likely how the ore was dumped in. In the distance, a heavy large wheeled vehicle rumbled. The back had a large rail-like protrusion, probably how the modules mounted on to it.

Jax watched the two power loaders move the cargo unit into position near the rail tracks. He tapped his chin as he thought. "Not for long, no. We'll have to figure something out." He took his gPhone out of his pocket and began snapping pictures, sending them back to the *Osprey* and the waiting Kori and Steve.

Naomi watched the men and women operating the loaders. "Bet twenty years ago, this whole place would have been automated. All droids."

"I don't think this colony existed twenty years ago, but yeah, almost certainly it would have been mostly droids." He turned his head to look at her. "Say what you will—and I have a lot to say about him—the emperor's hatred of droids and AI has pretty much zeroed out the unemployment rate." He scowled, thinking of the man responsible for his parent's deaths. "If someone wants to work, there's work to be had, somewhere."

"On a stinky mud planet, deep in a mine," Naomi replied. She looked at her companion from the corner of her eye. He hadn't said much about the Empire during their trip so far, and despite her admitting that she was the product of Imperial engineering, he didn't seem to be holding it against her.

Back on the *Osprey,* Steve's gPhone buzzed. He and Kori were on the common deck having a snack at the small table set against the bulkhead. Between them a tablet sat on the table with a schematic on it. Kori watched him take his gPhone and examine it. When Steve didn't immediately offer any details she said, "What? What's going on?" She leaned over to see his gPhone.

Steve offered his phone to her then stood. "Hey..." He looked at her. "What's the combat droid's name again?"

"Baxter," the speaker in the ceiling offered.

Steve looked up. "Thanks." He turned. "Hey, Baxter, care to join me in the hold? I want to work out some design ideas."

"I'm already in the hold," the droid replied, his voice coming from the stairwell.

LET'S MEET OUR MARK

Naomi walked back to the booth she and Jax had camped out in. She pointed to a middle-aged man sitting at a table in the middle of the bar with three other people, all wearing similar coveralls. The same logo they'd seen on the perimeter fence was stenciled on their backs. They had scoped out the depot for a while then asked around for the bar that depot workers preferred. This one was their second stop.

Naomi inclined her head. "The one with the loud laugh."

Jax leaned over to look past her just as the man in question released a guffaw that turned heads a few tables over. It seemed his laugh was well known. Several patrons turned to look, smiled, and returned to their business. He leaned back as Naomi sat down and grabbed her beer. "How you wanna handle this?" he asked. The two of them had hung around the outskirts of the depot, taking pictures and readings of everything they could until they'd spotted a group of people leaving the yard.

She looked over her shoulder a little, humming. She turned back to Jax. "What do we need from this guy?"

He swiped on the screen of his gPhone. Her own device beeped as the screen came to life. She picked her gPhone up and examined it. "Okay, I'll take a crack at it." She looked at him. "This is not because you suggested it, and I'm not sleeping with him." She pocketed her gPhone and stood up and left.

He watched her approach the table; their target, Adamic, and two other men and a woman all looked up and watched her arrive. She leaned on the table, making eye contact with Adamic. Jax sipped his beer, flagging down a server. When the young woman arrived, he said, "Another round please, and another order of onion rings." As the server turned he added. "These are onion, right? Not eel?" She made a face then turned and left.

Naomi laughed what Jax thought might be her flirtatious laugh. He wondered why she'd never tried that laugh on him. It might have worked better than breaking and entering. He watched her sit down with the group of depot workers.

Steve was standing in the cargo hold of the *Osprey*, hands on his hips, turning in a slow circle. He stopped to look at Baxter, who was standing off to the side, watching him. "Does the cargo door being open during flight interfere with anything?"

The combat droid didn't move but said, "I didn't design the ship."

"Do you know how much weight this winch assembly

can tolerate?" He pointed to the equipment mounted to the ceiling of the hold. The assembly could telescope out of the hold in order to bring cargo aboard.

Again, the droid didn't move. "No."

Steve sighed. "You're not very helpful." Kori chuckled, putting her hand over her mouth.

Finally, Baxter moved, shrugging his shoulders. "I'm a combat droid. You called me for help. I don't know anything about the technical details of the *Osprey*." The droid made a show of looking around. "If you have something heavy you'd like me to move, I'm your droid."

Steve sighed and looked at the ceiling. "Skip?"

"Yes, Steve?"

Steve rubbed his face as he groaned. "Have you heard the questions I asked Baxter?"

"I have," the ship's SI replied.

"And... and would you be able to answer them?"

"Yes."

"Goddamnit!" Steve screamed. "Now I know you're messing with me!" He looked at Kori. "This is probably why the emperor hates droids. They're dicks."

Baxter made a clucking noise that Steve guessed must be his laugh. The matte back combat droid and the ship's SI replied in unison, "We are."

Skip continued, "The design of the Valerian Co-op Infiltrator made cargo a secondary, at best, consideration. In fact, based on sales brochures from when this ship was in active production, the cargo hold was meant for crew use on extended missions. As such, opening the cargo doors during flight operations was not something factored into the design.

However, Jax has opened them on occasion during atmospheric flight, and while it impacts flight dynamics, it does not hamper flight. The space frame is rigid enough to handle the stress." Steve nodded along as the SI replied. He opened his mouth, but Skip continued, "As for the winch assembly, the carrying capacity is primarily impacted by the tensile strength of the line as the arms are integrated into the spaceframe. As such, each cargo arm can hold approximately fifty tons. Approximately." Steve looked up at the two telescoping arms and massive spools mounted horizontally next to each.

Steve pulled his gPhone out of his pocket and did some calculations. "Okay, so we'll definitely need to grab the cargo module and drop it somewhere, then come back for the other. Gonna make this much tighter." He looked around. "I bet we can brace the arms." He pointed to a section of the hold aft of him. "There." Then he pointed to the forward edge of each door. "And there." He tapped his phone, then his earpiece. He grunted, "Voicemail." He slid his phone back into his pocket.

Naomi walked back to the booth, grinning. Jax smiled and extended his hand to the beer he had waiting for her. "Get what we needed?"

She looked over her shoulder, Adamic smiled and waved. Two of his coworkers had left to play a game that involved a metal ring attached to a long string and a hook on a support pillar. They were swinging the ring, trying to get it onto the hook. She turned to Jax. "Turns out our new friend Tommy Adamic's interests don't align with," she gestured to her body, "this." Jax raised an eyebrow. She nodded. "Yup."

He leaned over to look past Naomi's slim figure. Adamic was smiling. "I see." He picked up his beer and drained it, then grabbed the fresh one he had ordered for Naomi and stood up. "Guess you might as well head back to the *Osprey*." He smiled. "Don't wait up." He walked toward the waiting stockyard foreman and his remaining colleague.

"We don't have forever," she reminded.

LET'S PLAN A HEIST

Kori and Steve were sitting on the lip of the open cargo hold, feet dangling over the edge, watching the city. Each had a beer in hand. Naomi had returned a few hours prior in a rental buggy like the one she and Jax had taken into town.

Jax arrived on foot. When he spotted his friends up above, he said, "The rental buggies shut off at night, apparently." He moved out of sight to the boarding ramp and stomped his feet to get rid of the mud that had accumulated, finally giving up and slipping his boots off.

When Jax arrived barefoot in the cargo hold, Kori winked, her brown eyes twinkling in the harsh overhead lighting of the hold. "Naomi said to not expect you until morning." Steve nudged her in the shoulder.

Jax smiled and winked. "Not everyone hits the sheets on the first date." Steve coughed. Jax added, "Every time." He gestured around to the world beyond the cargo hold. "Even if it'd be the most fun thing on this damp rock."

"You get what we needed?" Steve asked, his composure coming back. Jax nodded. "That's good." He turned to point to some recent modifications to the hold. "Check out what we've been up to." He pointed to the two powerful extending arms in the ceiling. "Kori and Baxter helped me reinforce each arm." He gestured to thick beams that had been welded to the arm assemblies and the deck in two places on each side: port and starboard. "We also ordered some reinforced cable, but it won't get delivered until tomorrow morning. Should be a quick install, though. Baxter can braid it for extra tensile strength."

Kori laughed, "That should fun to watch."

Jax nodded. "Great." He looked around. "Naomi sleeping?" Kori nodded. "Okay. We should all hit the sack, get a good night's sleep. We'll plan over breakfast." Steve and Kori both nodded.

Baxter stepped forward. "I'll go patrol." He turned his scatter light toward the open starboard cargo bay door.

Jax smiled. "Careful, it's muddy out there."

The droid grunted. "I was made for combat. A little mud won't bother me." He turned Kori, "After I braid the cable I can tackle your hair." Before she could reply, he continued to the lip and took a step dropping to the muddy landing area below. Both doors began to slide closed.

Kori looked at Jax, "No he did not just..." A hand absently reaching up to pat one of her afro puffs.

Jax shrugged and gestured to the staircase. He followed Kori and Steve up to the common area. The two headed to their bunks: Kori to the quarters she now shared with Naomi and Steve to the room previously occupied by Mr. Ichiko, next to Jax's captain's quarters. Jax stopped at the kitchen for a glass of water.

Rudy rolled over. "Skip tells me that everything went well." Jax nodded as he drank.

The rust-colored navigation droid rolled over to the

small charging station in the bulkhead next to the large entertainment screen. His head spun to look at Jax. "You okay?"

Jax smiled. "Yeah, all good. Just nerves before the job, I guess."

"Uh, huh," the droid said, noncommittally, "I'm sure that's it."

Jax stared at him a moment. "Shut up and charge." He headed for the hallway that led to the crew berths. As he passed the door to Steve's quarters, he knocked twice, then pressed the control on his own door. When he entered his berth, he left his door open.

The following morning Naomi and Kori walked into the kitchenette area. The ebony-skinned woman focused on setting the coffee maker to work. Her brightly colored fingernails were drumming against the machine impatiently.

A few minutes later, as both women chatted over their cups of coffee, Steve walked into the common area. "Morning, all." He rubbed his dark brown hair, then ran his hand down his face. He looked at the two women, their eyes boring holes in him. A blush crept up his neck to his cheeks, forcing him to turn toward the cupboard. He busied himself with fixing a cup of coffee.

Kori, tired of waiting for Steve to turn back around, said, "Good morning to you, too." Something in the way she said those five words caused Steve's cheeks to burn brighter. He was certain the back of his neck was on fire. He reached up into the cupboard to grab another coffee cup.

Jax walked in. "Morn—" Steve shoved a cup of coffee at him.

Both women turned their stares from Steve to a new target. Jax sipped the coffee, then looked at the two women. "What?"

Steve sidled towards the lounge area the long way around. Kori waggled her eyebrows but said nothing.

Jax turned and looked at Rudy, still in his charging port. "Rudy."

Rudy made a mechanical sound. "If the hormone parade is over." He disengaged from his charger and rolled to stand in front of the wall-mounted entertainment screen. "My understanding is that we need to get things planned." He turned to Steve. "They should deliver your order of cabling in thirty minutes. I'll have Baxter accept it." Steve nodded dumbly, looking from Jax to the droid and the two women, then the entertainment screen and finally to the ceiling. The ceiling held his attention the longest.

Once everyone had settled in, Jax said, "Okay, here's the deal. The train comes in tonight around five. It takes two hours to load it up. Thanks to my new friend Tommy Adamic, I know that for sure the lot numbers Ichiko gave me will be on this shipment. They've got loads from dozens of Co-ops and larger operations going out on this train." He looked around. "Bad news, we've got no idea where the lots will be. Tommy said it's semi random based on load balancing the cars. Not every module is loaded the same. The train engineer and load master provide a final layout when the loading is done and send that along to the yard managers in Salma."

Naomi held up her hand.

"Yes?" Jax nodded to her.

"You sure got the right lot numbers?"

Jax shrugged, producing his gPhone. "Data file Ichiko gave me. We'll have to check each car. The lot numbers are only visible from the walkways inside the cars." He took a breath. "The train is expected to be almost two klicks long, so we'll have to move fast."

"Not awesome," Steve said. "We're gonna have to move real fast. It shouldn't be hard to hack the locking mechanisms on those cars, but moving the modules off, then coming back for more, gonna take time."

Jax nodded. "Easier than you think. We'll head out after Stevie and Kori get the new cabling installed. I want to be at the staging area well before the train leaves the city." He turned to Rudy. "Speaking of, got someplace in mind?"

The small droid changed the density of his roller ball, allowing his body to bob up and down twice as he nodded with one fist. The main entertainment display showed an overhead map of the town of Abda and surrounding terrain. The GappleSoft logo was on the bottom right. He rolled to the display. "Here." A section of the map lit up with a red dot. "The train line," it lit up in blue, "runs right here, only a few kilometers away. When the train leaves Abda, we can be airborne and ready for intercept in minutes. This region is shielded from both cities by these hills. The *Osprey* coming and going won't attract attention."

Naomi clapped her hands loudly. "Let's go rob somebody!"

TOOT TOOT

The ore train arrived in Abda on schedule, right at five o'clock. Tommy Adamic watched the empty cars roll by until the three-kilometer train came to a stop. He lifted his gPhone to his ear. "Ready in zone two."

His colleague, the woman who was at the bar with him last night, replied, "Zone one ready." The two other men from his table replied, as well, all four loading zones were ready.

Adamic pocketed his gPhone and turned to the nearest power loader. "Chen, go ahead and get started."

"Roger that, Tommy," the man strapped into the yellow and black painted power loader standing nearby said before turning and joining another lifter to heft a massive cargo module onto the heavy loading arm of a crane that straddled the tracks. The crane was able to roll along the length of track inside the stockyard, loading the heavy ore modules onto the waiting train car frames. Men and women in power loaders all along the line were preparing cargo modules, loaded with delibdomin ore worth millions in Imperial credits, for the crane as it made its way along the track.

"The train just left the station," Rudy said, then added, "and it's three klicks long."

Jax swore under his breath, then nodded and tapped the intercom control. "Train is moving, so are we!" He closed the channel and pushed the grav-lift control forward, increasing power. The *Osprey* lifted off, its landing gear pulling out of the mud with a sucking sound. They had landed in a small clearing after Steve and Kori received their delivery of reinforced cable. Baxter had spent most of the morning braiding the thick cable to increase its strength.

Down in the cargo hold, Steve and Kori were checking each other's safety straps. The cargo hold doors on both sides of the *Osprey* were open, and Steve's reinforced cargo arms were fully extended. As the ground receded and the wind picked up, Kori shouted, "Ready?" She had pistols strapped to each of her legs. Despite Jax's teasing that she had no value among the crew, her aim was top-notch and not limited to darts.

She tugged on her own harness and walked over to the port side cargo opening. The ground, now two kilometers below them, was passing by quickly as the *Osprey* moved to get into position to intercept the train.

From their headsets, Jax said, "Once we get going, we'll have maybe two hours before the train is close enough to Salma for the local Imperials to engage."

Steve tapped his earpiece. "Roger that. We'll keep quiet. You sure your AI can fly this thing on its own?" He grinned.

Skip cut off Jax's reply. "One, I'm right here, and two, I fly better than Jax."

"Let's not get crazy," Jax cut in, then added, "but yeah, Skip has this."

The *Osprey* banked, and from the starboard cargo door, the view of the train line came into view. In the distance, the bright blue painted main engine of the train came around a bend, the kilometers-long ore train behind it.

Jax pushed away from his flight console as the controls slid into their standby position. He turned to Rudy. "You two do *got this*, right?"

Rudy made his nodding gesture. "Yeah, we got this."

Jax nodded and headed down the staircase. When he got to the common deck, he saw Baxter. "You ready?"

"Are you kidding? This has been the most boring job ever so far." The droid pounded a fist into his open palm. He led Jax down the stairs to the cargo hold. When they arrived, Kori handed Jax his harness, helping him into it.

Naomi leaned out the open cargo door. "Ready?" Everyone nodded. She tapped her earpiece. "Okay, droids, bring us into position."

"We have names," Rudy said over comms.

"Moving into position now," Skip interrupted. The *Osprey* dipped as she dived toward position over the tracks. Below them, the train's engine approached, then whizzed past underneath. The *Osprey* accelerated and was over the train in seconds, maintaining position. The ship lowered until it was barely twenty meters over the train.

"Uh, I think we have a problem," Skip said.

Everyone in the hold looked at each other. Jax said, "What's wrong?"

"There's a car in the middle of the train. It's not an ore car, and sensors can't penetrate it. It could be anything."

Naomi looked at Jax. "Your boyfriend mention anything about special cargo?"

Jax held up a finger. "One, not my boyfriend. Two, no, he didn't. I have to assume he didn't know. The train was coming in from the town further down the line. Could be anything." He looked around. "Rudy, can you pick up any chatter? I don't like not knowing what's in that thing."

"Scanning, now," the nav droid replied from his station on the flight deck. "Nothing. All comms on that train are hard-wired, and at least right now, they're not talking to anyone over wireless," the droid said.

"Damn." Jax looked around. "Okay, well, we stick to the plan. We'll drop on the last car and work our way forward. When we find the first car, Kori and Naomi will call down the *Osprey*. Baxter will get the car connected and they'll take off. Steve and I will keep going and find the second car. Rinse and repeat." He looked at Kori and Naomi. "You two ride out with the ore module. Baxter, you stay on the train in case we need you." Everyone nodded.

TEN

NO PLAN SURVIVES FIRST CONTACT

Baxter was the first down, not needing to be lowered by the cargo arms. When they were in position, he stepped off the edge of the cargo hold and plummeted to the train car below. The moment he landed on the train module, he magnetized his feet and began active scanning along the kilometers of cars ahead of him. He motioned the others down and stalked forward.

Jax and Steve came down first, the heavy-duty cable making a piercing whine as it unspooled aboard the *Osprey*, letting the two men mostly free fall until the last three meters. They unclipped quickly and headed toward the rear of the car at a crouch. The pale star that served as a sun for Jebidiah was setting. The cables retracted quickly so that Naomi and Kori could hook in and descend. They might have two hours before anyone spotted them, but the sun would be down long before that.

Once all five of them were on the ore car, they headed for the hatch at the rear end of the car. The platform in front of the door was not large, big enough for two people at most. Jax jumped down, careful to not fall backward off the car. He looked at the small control panel set in the door. "Looks straightforward. I couldn't get too many details out of my pal at the stockyard, but he mentioned that most of these cars are still set to factory specs, since no one actually cares to memorize security codes for hundreds of these modules." He looked up at his friends, "Once we crack one, should be easier after that." He looked at Naomi. "Right?"

Naomi jumped down and knelt next to the hatch and the control panel. After a minute of tinkering in which Jax noticed a familiar blue glow, she looked up. "Abra cadabra." The hatch popped and swung in. "Now that I know the default settings, it'll go faster." She said as she stood and entered the internal corridor of the train car.

As Steve jumped down to enter the car, he looked at the panel. "She's good. Can't even tell she messed with it."

Jax looked down. "Uh, yeah. Good." He shoved Steve inside to make room for Kori, who was sitting above them waiting to jump down to the small platform.

The ore modules sat atop the barebones train car. Without modules, the car would resemble a flatbed with framed in walkway running down the center. The ore modules, shaped like a squat upside down U, rested over the walkway and locked into the car with thick latches along the sides at the front and back of the car. Each car could hold two modules.

The walkway was surrounded by a rigid framework that fit into grooves in the modules to provide a bit more stability.

In the middle of each car was a small display mounted to the mesh of the walkway. It displayed which lot number the two ore modules corresponded to.

Jax looked at the small device. "Not so lucky, not this car." He motioned for the group to continue. Due to his height, Baxter had stayed topside, pacing them from above, and keeping an eye out for trouble.

As they neared the hatch that would lead to the next train car, Rudy called in, "How's it going?" Their comms were short range only, good for maybe a kilometer at best, less with tons of delibdomin between them and the Valerian Infiltrator keeping position overhead.

"We just got here. Car one is a bust," Jax growled. From the inside, it was easy to unlock the hatch and move across the narrow walkway that connected the cars. The tracks rattled past below. Naomi moved gingerly past Jax to look at the next hatch. She knelt down, careful to keep her body between the control panel and the others. It took half as long as the first to open. Jax said, "Hold tight. We'll signal you when we find it."

The second car was a bust. So were the third and fourth. Kori said from the back of their procession, "You're sure this the right train?"

"It's the only train," Jax grated, then added, "We've barely covered the first quarter of cars, but you're right in that we gotta pick up the pace." He shoved Steve, who had taken the lead of the group so the other man would jog the length of the car.

They checked two more cars before finding the first of two lot numbers Jax had been given. "This is it," he said. "According to Ichiko, this is one of the lots that were stolen from his Co-op by the neighboring much larger mining corporation." He motioned to Kori and Steve. "You two remember the drill on the latching mechanism?"

Kori had her hair in tight braids. They swayed as she nodded. "Attach the bypass doodad you gave us, clip to the blue wire, then cut."

"Green. Green wire," Steve replied, sighing.

"Oh, right. Green." Kori grinned. She batted her eyelashes, her brown eyes gleaming in the dim light. "I got this."

Steve reached for the device but was blocked expertly. "I'll do it. You head to the rear. You'll see when the latches disengage." Steve frowned, then nodded.

Kori looked at Jax and Steve, then kissed Jax on the cheek. "Good luck." She looked at Naomi. "Keep him safe." The slimmer Japanese woman inclined her head.

Jax shook his head. "Come on, let's get to the next car so these two can get out of here." He tapped his earpiece. "Found one, standby." Then, he turned back to his friends. "Remember, we want both modules. Don't disconnect them!" Jax shouted. Kori and Steve gave a thumbs up.

"Standing by," Skip replied.

After Jax and Naomi moved to the next car, Kori leaned out over the narrow connector walkway. The latch controls were meant to be accessed by stockyard personnel, standing on the ground, next to the unmoving train. The ground roared by barely a foot from her head as she strained to reach the control panel. One of her braids skittered across the gravel that raced by underneath. Absently, she thought about the fact that the train line was sitting on gravel, and given how muddy that part of the planet was, it must have taken a lot of work to get all that gravel in one place. The wiring connected each car to the control center in the engine. The bypass would keep telling the control system that the ore modules were latched to the car like normal. The bypass device would release the two modules, keeping them connected to each other with long bars that slide along the exterior creating a rigid structure.

Using her legs to push further under the train car, while clutching the railing with one hand, she managed to open the control panel, revealing the control lever for the latches and the signal wires. She attached the bypass and cut the green wire. The small LED on the bypass blinked twice, then remained lit. She exhaled a breath she hadn't realized she was holding and flipped the switch.

As she pulled herself back up onto the connector walkway, she heard the metallic clang of the latches built into the car disengaging from the cargo module. Up above, as the latches disengaged, large metal loops meant for the heavy duty crane at the stockyards slid up and out of the ore module. By the time Kori climbed up to the top of the module, Baxter had secured the harness that Steve designed to both ends of the module. It was now nearly pitch black. Each member of the team had a night vision visor. She pulled hers down over her eyes to see Baxter standing a meter away. Steve was at the far end of the train, his side attached to the frame. The matte black combat droid walked past her and effortlessly leapt to the next car in the line. When he landed, he said over comms, "See you both soon."

There was a metallic twang as the reinforced cable went taut, the *Osprey* using her powerful grav-lifts to pull the ore module off the train car.

The *Osprey* rocked and her engine noise ratcheted up a couple of decibels as she tilted wildly. "Okay, this is harder than I expected," Skip said over the speakers.

Rudy was gripping his console, even though his roller ball was magnetically secured to deck. The smart material had flattened a bit so more surface was in contact with the deck. "Yeah, you don't seem to be doing a good job at this."

The *Osprey* tilted the opposite direction. "What's the problem? You've piloted the *Osprey* hundreds of times over the years."

"Of course, but never with such a heavy load dangling underneath, messing with the flight dynamics," the ship's SI replied. "Hold on." The ship shuddered and banked.

"I am," Rudy replied. "We need to hurry."

"I know that."

"Then why are you not heading in the right direction?"

The ship lurched and tilted wildly. "My bad."

SO FAR SO GOOD, SORTA

Jax and Naomi were four, maybe five—they'd lost count—
ore cars from the car they'd left the others in. They were at
the hatch to the car that was coupled to the mystery car that
was blocking the *Osprey's* sensors. Rudy and Skip had thus
far had no luck picking up any transmissions from the
train's engine or anywhere else on the train prior to
departing with Steve and Kori and their first ore module.

Naomi was doing her glowy blue interface thing on the
locking mechanism when the lock clicked and the hatch
swung in, to reveal a bored looking shock trooper. "Oh
hell!" Jax said, pulling the shocked woman to the side of the
hatch as the trooper shouted something and raised his
carbine.

Blaster bolts shot through the open hatch to score the
car behind them. Jax leaned in and returned fire. He looked
at Naomi. "We can't let him call this in!" He leaned out to
fire again, and this time, Naomi crouched and then bolted
through the hatch, tackling the shock trooper. Jax groaned
and charged in behind her, leaping onto the free arm of the
armored man fighting with his small attacker. Glowing blue

attacker, Jax noticed. As Jax struggled, he swatted at his ear. "Rudy! Are you back? I need you to jam all comms!" Naomi wriggled and generally kept the trooper busy as she tried to hold on to his helmet, her hand lined with glowing blue tattoos.

"Grab his comm gear!" Naomi shouted.

Jax reached for the trooper's equipment belt, ripping the comm gear off, breaking the connection to the armor in a shower of sparks.

"We're almost done dropping the ore module off," Rudy replied. Jax growled but didn't reply. He was still busy with the armored man underneath him.

The trooper pushed Naomi up and away as he slammed a fist into Jax's midsection, driving the air from his lungs. In a flash of black hair and blue jumpsuit, Naomi was back, clinging to the back of the still sitting trooper, trying to force the man's helmet off. Her hands, and what was visible of her arms, were glowing brightly. Jax couldn't tell what she was doing, but it must have been distracting.

Jax finally came to his senses and pushed his pistol under the struggling trooper's arm and fired once, then again. The armored man slumped and stopped thrashing. Smoke wafted up from a glowing burn hole in his armor under his right arm where the armor was weak.

Jax gestured to the logo of the grand human Empire on the hatch leading to the mysterious train car. "Guessing that's full of these guys." He hitched a thumb over his shoulder toward the dead trooper inside the car behind them.

Naomi made a face. "You think?" She looked at the hatch. "What do you wanna do?"

"We can't take an entire train car of shock troops."

"I can," Baxter said from the roof of the car behind them. The two humans turned to look up at the matte black combat droid, or at least his red optical scanner scatter light as it swished back and forth. The rest of him blended in with the moonless night. The droid stepped off the car, landing with a thud on the walkway before them. "You two, up and over. I can jam comms within a small radius. I'll take care of our Imperial friends."

"This train pulling into the station full of dead shock troops won't be subtle," Naomi pointed out.

The combat droid shrugged. "Neither will it pulling in missing two entire cars' worth of ore modules."

Jax smiled. "Point, the combat droid. Still, an ore theft is one thing. Slaughtering what must be an entire company," he said as he scrambled up the rungs to the roof of the Imperial troop car, "is a whole other thing."

Naomi knelt next to the control panel, her hand resting on it. The blue biological circuitry tattoos lit up briefly, then faded. She looked up, winked, then followed him up the ladder to the roof of the military transport car.

Baxter climbed up the ladder of the car connected to the military car. "I'll have to wait here. I'm certain they'd hear my heavy ass stomping along the top of their car."

Jax looked over. "Good call. We'll hurry." The combat droid nodded and crouched down.

AND THEN, SIDEWAYS

"Jax." It was Skip. "We're on site, be over you in a second."

Naomi looked around until she finally caught sight of the lift engines burning.

From below the train car, Jax said, "Good job, buddy." He was dangling from the connecting walkway between two cars. They had found the second and final ore two cars up train from the Imperials.

Rudy's voice crackled. "You have to hurry. The train is getting close to the *oh no* zone. Like really close. Be on station in thirty seconds."

Naomi cut in, "You ready?" She was standing atop the car, watching the *Osprey* approach.

Jax replied, "Yup, activating bypass now." The control panel was open, and he connected the bypass device. The LED was solid. He cut the wire and the LED on the bypass device went out. He stared at the device, then slammed his palm on the side of it. Nothing.

"All good?" Naomi asked. "Our ride's here."

Jax stared at the cut wire and the presumably broken or malfunctioning bypass device and its criminally dark LED.

"Oh well, yeah, more or less." He reached for the lever, turned it, then hoisted himself back up onto the platform. "Let's get this done." Above him the *Osprey roared* overhead. The sound of locking latches along both sides of the car releasing was faint over the roar of wind and clickity-clack of the train.

When he climbed to the top of the ore car, Naomi already had the makeshift harness connected to his end of the car. The *Osprey* had flown up the length of the train, picking up Baxter along the way. The combat droid was connecting the harness to the loop on the end closest to Jax. The droid turned. "You broke something, didn't you?" Naomi looked up, eyebrow raised.

"What makes you say that?" Jax held up a hand. "You know what? Not now." He looked at Naomi, who gave a thumbs up, then looked up at the *Osprey*. "Skip, let's—"

The module lurched, throwing Naomi out of view at the far end of the train car. Jax barely held on. The module began to rise. He didn't hesitate; he turned and leapt from his position at the opposite end of the module to the car below.

"What the hell are you doing?" Baxter demanded over the comms. He was standing magnetically affixed to the center of the module, directing Skip.

"Jax!" Baxter said. Over the comms, it was hard to tell, but for a second, Jax thought he heard concern in the normally stoic combat droid.

"Naomi fell off," Jax said. He had landed with a thud on the small connecting platform between cars.

"I'm okay," she reported. He couldn't see her. She was somewhere below the now exposed walkway that ran the length of the empty ore car.

"Jax, I think the jig is up," Skip said.

Rudy added, "Yeah, you did something. I've got encrypted comms coming and going from that troop transport car."

"I'm picking up life signs, too. Those shock troops are spreading out from their car up and down train," Skip said, then added, "And I've got what look like two shuttles inbound from Salma."

"Head to the staging area, finish the job. They'll spot you in seconds!" Jax ordered. "We're not supposed to meet with Ichiko's people until," he looked at the old wrist watch he wore, "tonight. That's plenty of time for things to cool off. Naomi and I will lie low and find a ride to you or wait and let you come get us," Jax said as he started toward where Naomi was, which had the added benefit of being away from the Imperial shock troops that were making their way up train.

The *Osprey* continued to rise and banked away from the train. "Stay safe, you idiot," Kori said over comms.

When he reached Naomi, she was nursing her right leg. "You okay?"

"We'll hide?" she asked.

He shrugged. "I said *or something*." He pointed to her leg. "You walk?" He extended an arm to help her up.

She reached up. "Yeah, I think it's just twisted." She eased up and tested her weight on the foot. She looked up at Jax. "Yeah, I'll be fine." She smiled. "Another upside of being an interface, healing nanites."

"Sweet," Jax said, then looked toward the rear of the train. Somewhere a few cars away were Imperial shock troops. He turned back to the smaller woman. "We gotta go." He gestured to the control panel. She knelt down and unlocked the hatch. They both rushed in and closed the hatch behind them.

Naomi looked around. "Thoughts?"

Jax walked further inside the train. He was tapping his chin as he turned in a slow circle, looking around the narrow caged-in walkway. "Your blue glowy power, that's touch based, right?"

"Blue glowy?" the slender woman repeated. She shook her head. "Yeah, I have to be in physical contact." Jax nodded and continued to look around. She turned toward the hatch leading further up the train. "Should we keep moving forward?"

Jax shook his head. "No real point. Eventually we'll hit the engine, then what?"

Naomi leaned against the side of the walkway and slid to the ground. "They'll kill us if they catch us." She looked up. "You know that, right?"

Jax smirked. "You're the one that literally forced your way into this."

She returned the expression. "I didn't *literally* force anything. But yeah, I get it." She stamped her foot against the floor of the narrow walkway. It made a hollow thud sound. Jax turned and looked at her. She looked up. "What?"

He rushed over and knelt down, shoving her aside. "There's a hatch here."

"Hey!" she shouted. "You could have just asked me to move."

He looked over. "Sorry." He turned his attention back to the hatch in the floor. They were standing a few feet from the center of the train car. He ran his hand along the hatch, looking for a locking mechanism or something that would open the hatch. He looked at Naomi. "Can you do your—"

"Glowy blue thing?" she completed, her eyebrow raised.

203

She got to her feet and moved next to him, resting her hand on it. The blue lines began to glow.

"I was gonna say *magic,* but yeah," Jax said, his eyes on hers.

The hatch sprang open between them. Naomi smiled. "Still never sleeping with you." She removed her gPhone from her pocket and hefted the hatch open. She turned on the flashlight and peered inside. She looked at Jax. "Must be mechanical access." Inside the hatch was a maze of pipes and pistons. Several were moving as the train car shifted back and forth. "Be a tight, and greasy, fit."

Jax consulted his gPhone. "Less than an hour to Salma." He leaned over to look inside the mechanical area, then turned and looked at Naomi. "No choice." He extended an arm toward the small opening. Naomi groaned and lowered her way down into the narrow crawl space.

Jax followed and pulled the hatch shut.

ELEVEN

NOW WE WAIT

"So, what now?" Steve asked from his place sitting on the spiral staircase that ran up through all three levels of the Valerian Co-op Infiltrator.

Kori shrugged. "Like Jax said, we sit here with the modules. Wait for the client to come pick 'em up. The sun will be up in..." She trailed off.

Skip volunteered, "Half an hour, -ish."

"-Ish?" Steve asked, looking at the ceiling.

"I'm a spaceship, not a clock."

Rudy chimed in, "We're almost at the drop off. For what it's worth, I agree, we should drop the ore module with the other one, then wait for the client. Once that's done, we can head to Salma. They have the large spaceport anyway, will be easy to get a landing clearance."

Kori nodded. She had to grab a railing set in the bulkhead near where she was standing to keep her balance. "Yeah. Jax can take care of himself, and it sounds like Naomi is even more capable." She thought for a minute. "Just to confirm, those shuttles aren't onto us, right?"

Skip made a laughing, clucking kind of sound. "I'd

expect you to know better, Kori. No base shuttle is going to track me, unless I want it to."

"Lotta ego for an AI," Steve said, standing to head up to the common deck.

From his position on the module swaying below the *Osprey*, Baxter beamed, *I like it better when it's just Jackson. These two talk too much.*

Agreed, Rudy and Skip beamed back at the same time.

The sound of heavy boots thudded above the small hatch.

Jax looked at Naomi in the faint glow of their combined gPhone screens. "These mechanicals, plus the ore, should make us nearly impossible to detect." He paused as someone stomped by overhead. "At least with the gear these guys likely have."

"You think those shuttles brought in gear or tech?" Naomi asked. She'd managed to smudge one side of her face with purple-ish dust from the ore in the modules above. It seemed to find its way everywhere. It covered every surface of the crawl space they were hiding in.

"I can't imagine. They were probably dispatched to see if any ships or ground vehicles were nearby. The bypass didn't work, something went wrong, so the engine crew got an alert. I'm sure they know the ore is gone, but I'm guessing they can't investigate until the train arrives in Salma. Lot of companies and Co-ops will be clamoring for their ore."

The train car bumped along and rumbled. The sound of shock troopers moving around in the narrow walkway overhead had subsided. Naomi looked at her phone. "Should we get out?" She tried to twist into a more comfortable position, unsuccessfully.

Jax shook his head. He'd given up trying to sit in the low clearance space. He was lying on his back, hands behind his head. "I think we should wait. When the train pulls into the Salma stockyard, it'll be bustling with activity. We can sneak out then." He took a breath. "I think."

"You think?"

He turned to look the woman in the eye. "Look, girl-friend, I'm a lot of things: smuggler, occasional pirate—though rarely—freight hauler, a bounty hunter, once—but that was more an accident—private security." He held up a finger. "Secret agent, never been on the list." He smirked. "Or ninja, though that'd be pretty cool. I'd sign up to be a ninja."

She looked at him for a minute, then sighed. "Maybe being your partner isn't a good idea."

Jax blinked several times. "Uh, I never offered you a partnership."

She winked. "You would, eventually. I'm persuasive." When he got a look on his face, she said, "Not like that, you horn dog."

Jax leaned back, both hands held up. "Woah."

She raised a purple dust smudged eyebrow. "In the short time I've known you, I've found out that sleeping with anyone of poor taste or decision-making skills is right near the top of your skills list." She grinned. "Above smuggler."

"I can't help being dashingly handsome."

She laughed loud enough that she clamped a hand over her mouth, her eyes darting left and right, making sure no one had heard her.

Jax eyed the woman next to him that he barely knew. "So, we've got time. What's your deal?"

COMING CLEAN

Naomi inhaled. "What do you want to know? I told you about the interface program."

Jax nodded slowly. "Yeah. I got that part. You're an Imperial—" He held up a hand to stop her impending interruption. "—Former Imperial agent of some type. Meant to counter the Indie's use of droids and AI for hacking and intelligence gathering. What else?"

"Like my family history or something?" Jax nodded. She sighed, shifting again to find a comfortable position. "I mean it's nothing overly exciting. I was born on Shinchaku Hokkaido. My parents, too. Gran and Papa emigrated from Earth when they were newly married. They wanted to worship as they pleased."

"Religious pilgrims?" Jax asked, surprised.

"Shinchaku Hokkaido is more religiously tolerant than Japan on Earth. My grandparents—well, my family—are Catholic."

Jax was silent a moment. "My Memaw was pretty religious. My folks weren't, and I guess I'm even less."

The Japanese woman smiled. "The joys of space: plenty

of room for everyone." She watched the man opposite her for a few heartbeats as he thought over what she'd just told him. "And you? I mean, I dug up a lot on Kelso, but that only covered the founding of the station, forward. Where'd your grandparents come from?" She shifted again, hoping to find a maybe less uncomfortable position in the tight space. A piston near her shook slightly as it adjusted to something the train car was doing.

"You know, I don't know a whole lot. Memaw was never big on family history. I know she was a..." He tapped his chin, then shifted to a different lump of ore, then shifted again until he was comfortable. "...Protestant, I think. Never met my grandfather. He was out of the picture by the time Memaw helped found Kelso. She never talked about him. Not sure if he was dead or what." He paused, remembering back to his childhood before the war. "Dad only talked about him a few times, usually to use as an object lesson: *Don't be like your grandfather. Brush your teeth.* If you believed my dad, my grandpa had horrible teeth, never washed his face, and only took showers on days that started with W." He grinned, remembering his father doing his best to coax a young and stubborn Jackson into the bath.

The train car rocked as it passed over a small rise. Pistons hissed at each end of the car. When the rolling was done, Jax wiped his hands on his shirt. "I think I'll be burning everything I have on when we get back to the *Osprey*."

Naomi nodded her agreement, then said, "I saw in the Kelso station computer that your parents were Independents?"

Jax nodded. "Yeah, pretty high up. Memaw and the other founders of Kelso were intensely staunch supporters of the Independent Systems Alliance and its core principles. She raised Dad to be a lot like her, and when the war kicked off, Mom and Dad signed up. Left me on Kelso with Memaw." He rubbed his eyes, trying to make it look like he wasn't wiping a tear away. "Stupid ore dust. Getting my eyes."

Naomi snorted. "Yeah, dust."

Jax gave her a look. "Anyway, they both died near the end of the war. Memaw kept raising me until she died. Cancer. By that time, I was old enough to take care of myself, and Kelso isn't that big of a station, so folks looked out for me. Governor Singh was a good friend of Memaw's so she looked after me early on."

"I'm sorry." She put a hand on his knee. "That sounds rough."

He shrugged. "I've had a while to work through it." He looked at her hand on his knee, and she withdrew it like she had been electrocuted. "What about yours? Parents, I mean?"

"They weren't freedom fighters, that's for damn sure. They were, are, programmers." The look on her face told Jax a lot. "I haven't seen them since I entered the interface program."

"How come? Did they not approve?"

She sighed, closing her eyes. "They didn't—probably still don't—know. They're AI researchers. Some of the best. When the war started, they were conscripted by the emperor."

Jax rubbed his ear. "I don't understand. Why would that AI-hating Luddite conscript AI researchers?" She opened her mouth to answer, but he cut her off. "The purge?"

She nodded. "By then, of course, the war was over, the

interface program had been scrapped, and most of us were dead."

"Dead?" Both of his eyebrows were as high as physically possible on his forehead.

"Would you want a bunch of living intel gatherers wandering around? Especially ones that may not have exactly volunteered?"

"You were conscripted," he surmised.

"Yup. I know now that he was planning the purge all along, whether he won or not. They told me my parents would be imprisoned if I didn't join the interface program." She inhaled deeply, coughed once, then said, "I'm sure they were told I'd be killed if they didn't Co-operate." She shrugged. "I've been on the run since: odd jobs, lying low, like at the relief camp. Stuff like that ever since."

LYING LOW

"We're sealed up," Skip said over the ceiling speakers. "I've dialed up our sensor jamming, but our two ore modules are obviously visible if that search shuttle gets too close."

"It's still out there?" Kori asked. They had landed nearly thirty minutes ago, just before sunrise. She and Steve were sitting at the small two-person dining table. They had brewed a pot of coffee just after landing.

"Yeah," the *Osprey's* SI replied. "We're not in any immediate danger. This little valley is pretty well protected, and that shuttle is an older Mark Seven transport. Those don't have the best sensors."

Steve looked at the ceiling. "Okay, we'll have to hope that shuttle doesn't come this way."

Kori walked over. "If that shuttle does get close enough to see the ore modules, what then?"

Steve shrugged. "I guess we run and hope Jax can afford to refund that Ichiko guy." When Kori made a face, he added, "Honestly, no clue. Let's just do our best to make sure that doesn't happen."

Rudy dropped down the center of the stairwell. "We should get the ore modules covered, just in case. With the sun up, any ship in orbit or a satellite will spot the modules."

Steve crossed his arms. "By 'we,' you mean us and not you?"

Rudy held his slim mechanical arms, then pointed at his roller ball. "Whatever helps you get your ass outside." He turned and rolled back to the stairwell. As he zipped up the center of the stairs, he added, "Baxter can help."

Kori looked between Steve and Baxter, who was standing near the staircase. "I guess we should get out there." She stood and headed for the staircase, coffee cup in hand.

Steve looked at Baxter as he stood. The droid just stared at him, red scatter light swishing back and forth.

The ore module shifted as the train car lurched to a stop. The sound and vibration of the cars further down the line clanging against the car in front of them echoed.

Jax put his gPhone in his pocket and sat up, straining to press his ear against the hatch.

"Do you—" Naomi started.

"Shh," Jax rasped. She slapped him on the shoulder. He looked back and nodded. He pressed against the metal hatch, pushing it up. He poked his head out, then lowered it. "Clear."

"Well, if it wasn't, you'd be dead already," Naomi snapped, pushing against him.

"Okay, okay. Jeez." He crawled up and out and offered her his hand. They stood looking around the dimly lit walkway. Their car or another nearby clanked as a crane similar to the one in Abda began removing modules, handing them off to people in power loaders. "Here's what I'm thinking. We get out, and get under the car."

"And then?" Naomi pressed.

Jax made a face. "Do I have to think of everything?" He jumped back just in time to avoid a fist aimed at his shoulder.

Naomi turned to the hatch up train from them. "Let's go." She didn't wait for him.

Getting under the train car was the easy part by far. The Salma stockyard was a hive of activity, a kicked over hive at the moment, due to the theft of several million credits worth of raw ore. Shock troopers were stomping all over the yard, their gray armor covered in the all-too-common Jebidiah mud. Yard workers were scurrying around trying to do their job of unloading the train cars while not getting in the shock troopers' way. Mixed in with that were several haughty Imperial officers in crisp crimson uniforms barking orders at anyone who looked like they would follow them.

Jax and Naomi were crouched behind one of the massive sets of wheels at the end of the train car they'd been in. As yet, no one had even glanced in their direction.

"Would it be rude to ask, *now what*, again?" the runaway interface said.

"Rude and unnecessary," Jax replied without looking over at her, his eyes scanning the scene around the train.

Unlike Adba, where the train pulled along the perimeter of the stockyard, in Salma, the train pulled right into the middle of the much larger yard. The spaceport ring wall was visible in the distance, freighters moving in and out of the port on powerful lift engines.

Jax finally looked at Naomi. "Think they're looking for signals? We could call the others, have them meet us at the spaceport."

She shook her head. "No idea. Probably best to wait until we're at least outside the stockyard." Jax nodded.

TWELVE

SETTLING IN AND RUNNING

"Okay, no! No, not like that!" Rudy shouted over comms.

Steve turned and looked toward the *Osprey* parked fifty meters from them. Rudy was barely visible in the transparent titanium windows of the flight deck. He was gesticulating about something.

Kori looked at the half meter square contraption between her and Steve, then looked over to the ship. "What's the problem?"

"If you don't get it set in just the right place, you may not get full coverage," the droid insisted.

Kori had her hands on her hips. "It's almost noon. So, maybe, you know, we go for mostly covered versus perfectly covered." In the distance, the engines of the searching shuttle whined.

Steve looked at her, smiling. Rudy said, "Fine, fine. Who needs perfect when humans are involved?" The droid vanished from sight.

Steve leaned over and pressed a button on the device between them. A countdown started. He looked at it, then Kori. "We're sure it's pointed the right way?"

Kori was already moving toward the end of the module and the ladder there. Over her shoulder, she said, "Little late to worry about that." She vanished over the side of the module.

The younger Delphino looked at the device again. He reached down and quickly rotated the device ninety degrees. He backed away, then rushed back. The timer was at ten seconds. He turned again and ran to the device, turning it back to its original orientation. Five seconds. He looked at the end of the ore module, then turned and ran to the edge and leapt off. There was a pop followed by the sound of unspooling wire and ruffling fabric.

Steve had bought the devices back on Kelso Station. During the trip out, he had tinkered with them to see how they worked, at least as best he could without activating one. They contained a compressed gas canister and several dozen meters of memory metal wire. There was also a small power cell and several hundred square meters of fabric that, when charged, absorbed most conventional sensor radiation. The memory metal had been shaped to the specifications of the ore modules, courtesy of schematics provided by Mr. Ichiko. The older man couldn't be certain of the exact model of the modules, but he was fairly certain. The gas propelled the fabric and its wire frame out in all directions. It almost caught up to Steve before he hit the ground and rolled with a not at all dignified grunt.

Seconds later, the power cell engaged and the memory metal snapped into shape, wrapping the ore module completely.

Steve got back to his feet and said, "See, it was set up correctly."

Kori was already following behind Baxter, who was carrying the final device toward the other ore module.

"If you could hurry it up a little, that'd be excellent," Skip said. "Those shuttles look like they're working a pattern, and I'm guessing we'll be at the edge of their sensor range in another half hour or so."

Baxter, sensor mesh device in hand, leapt to the top of the ore module. As Kori climbed the ladder built into the end, she said, "You think they'll get close enough for visual?"

Rudy answered, "Probably not. We've been watching their pattern as best we can with the passive arrays. We're pretty far from the train line, and this valley isn't very big. They're probably assuming that they're looking for freighters."

Steve chimed in as he climbed up the module, "Still a good idea to make sure large metallic objects don't show up on their scopes where none should be."

"Go, now!" Jax hissed, watching a pair of shock troopers turn and head away from the train toward a small tent that they'd watched officers come and go from for almost an hour.

Naomi crawled out from under the car and took off in a running crouch. She covered the distance between the train car and an unattended ground cart quickly.

While they waited for an opportunity, they had settled on a plan that both felt had the best chance of them not being captured, arrested, and killed by Imperial forces. Neither thought it was a particularly good plan, but with nothing but their phones and a pistol each between them, it was their best bet.

Jax bolted from their hiding spot as soon as Naomi

reached the cart. In seconds, she had the cart's systems over-ridden and they were moving at what they hoped was a casual-looking pace towards the main administration building.

As the cart neared the building, a garage door automatically opened. Jax drove into the garage and parked the cart next to a half dozen similar carts. There was no one in the garage. By their best guess, the morning shift had already started and the night shift looked to have been kept on to help with the train heist investigation. "Let's find the locker room." He headed toward the personnel door, Naomi in tow. She placed her hand on the access card reader. Her blue tattoos lit up from fingertip to elbow, then faded as the small light on the device turned green and the door slid open.

The administration building was two stories, almost entirely empty. Occasionally they heard voices, usually near staircases up to the second floor, likely where managers were overseeing things from. Jax and Naomi split up to raid the men's and women's locker rooms.

After a rushed shower and a few looted lockers, Jax walked out of the men's locker room. "Orange is your color," Naomi said as she joined Jax in the anteroom outside the two locker rooms. Both were in bright orange jumpsuits with reflective strips on the arms and legs. Jax did a slow spin. She looked around, ignoring him. "What now?"

Jax shrugged. "Well, I'm hoping we can walk right out the front gate." He checked his gPhone. "Breakfast?" Naomi nodded.

THERAPY OR SOMETHING

The last of the camouflage nets deployed with the pop hiss of the compressed air driving the memory metal and smart fabric over the bundled ore modules. Kori and Steve, standing on either side of Baxter, smiled. Kori wiped her brow. She had pulled her hair back into a single puff near the back of her head. "How is it so muddy here if it gets this warm?"

Steve looked around. "Beats me. Let's head in, the ship has AC." He put a hand to his stomach. "And I'm starving."

Baxter was following behind them. "I'll patrol out here, make sure no one stumbles onto our little hiding place." Both humans nodded. The stoic combat droid loped off on a course away from the *Osprey*.

As they entered the cargo and continued up the staircase, Kori said, "So, what's the deal? You two get your shit worked out?"

Steve blushed. "Not really something I want to discuss with my brother's girlfriend."

"Prude." She chuckled as she started rifling through the cupboards and pantry looking for lunch fixings. "When we get back to Kelso, I'm gone. Marshall is fun and all, but it's not a long-term thing. You and Jax are both adults. No one is judging your choices."

Steve dropped into one of the chairs at the small dining table. He cleared his throat, then did it twice more. "It's not that...well, maybe." He looked at the ceiling. "This is kinda new to me."

Kori turned. "What, dating? Sex?" She smiled so widely that Steve leaned back. "You're not a virgin, are you?" She chuckled, "Well, I guess I know the answer to that one."

Steve shook his head. "No, but would that be so bad?"

Kori held up both hands, palms out. "Not at all." She turned back to the frying pan she'd started heating. She grabbed two eggs, cracking them as she spoke. "Nothing wrong with saving yourself. Sorry I laughed. You okay with breakfast for lunch?"

"Like I said, not a virgin, at least not like that. Jax is, well..." He trailed off, looking at his feet.

Kori put a few strips of bacon next to the sizzling eggs, then looked at the younger Delphino brother. "Oh. I see." She walked over and put her hand on his shoulder. "You know there's nothing wrong, right?" She looked over her shoulder and rushed back to flip the bacon and the eggs. "I mean, we like what we like, and that can, and does, change over time. Nothing to be ashamed of." She turned. "If your brother has an issue, I'll make sure he's squared away before I head home."

Steve looked up. "Yeah, I know, but...well, it's new." He watched her shuffle the bacon around. "Jax is a good guy, despite being a jerk to Marsh and me almost his entire life, growing up." He was silent a moment. "And no, despite that, Marsh isn't a problem. He's never been anything but open-minded and supportive."

"I seem to recall you Delphinos doing your part in that little rivalry thing with Jax," Kori quipped, sliding the eggs onto a plate. The bacon was still sizzling and spitting. "You guys were pretty mean to him when his parents died."

"Well, we were kids," Steve said as he stood and took the plate of eggs from Kori, putting it on the table. He moved to the refrigerator, looking inside. "Milk okay? Gross, why does he have skim milk?" He left the jug in the fridge and poured two glasses of water.

Kori slid the bacon onto another plate and sat down at the small table. As she redistributed the eggs and bacon across the two plates, she said, "So, if it's not what others think that's bothering you, what is? I can tell you, Jax is a pretty okay boyfriend."

Steve took a bite of bacon. After swallowing, he said, "That's...that's not exactly a great endorsement."

Kori shrugged. "Men are dumb. One, maybe two, in a hundred of you make good boyfriends or husbands. The rest are really just there for entertainment." She winked.

"I guess I just don't know what I want." He took a few bites of eggs. "These are good." She nodded, her eyes never leaving his. "That fight we had, when he came to Marsh and me about this?" He waved his free hand around to take in the *Osprey*. "We'd gone out a few times. Nothing serious, I thought. I was seeing a girl from station engineering. We had broken up rather spectacularly." He paused, weighing how much he wanted to share. "I was drowning my sorrows in Wendy's and Jax was down there closing a deal or something. We got to talking and one thing led to—"

Kori held up a hand. "I don't need details."

Steve made a face. "I wasn't going to give you any. Anyway, a few days later, Daisy and I patched things up, at least that's what I thought then. I told Jax. He thought I'd slept with him as a spite move or rebound or something. I got mad and accused him of seducing and taking advantage of me…" He trailed off, then added, "And I slugged him." He took a sip of his water. "Anyway, that was the last we'd talked until the dart tournament at the *Angry Spacer*."

"Yikes," Kori said between bites of egg. "Well, you know I like Jax, even having dated him for a while, but if you're thinking of exploring this aspect of your life, he's not the one I'd pick as a guide. You deserve better."

"Tell me about it. Seems like he'll sleep with anyone." He smiled as he ate a piece of bacon.

"He's not what I'd call choosy, no," Kori agreed.

EGGS AND BACON

They were walking with a group of night shift stockyard workers who were heading home, or to a bar. They'd barely gotten out of the admin building before hundreds of workers flooded into it as their shift finally ended, hours later than normal, thanks to the train robbery. They watched from behind a heavy lift ground transport as the night shift clocked out and headed for the gate to the stockyard, falling in towards the end of the group.

The exit to the yard was only a hundred meters away. A small turnstile was all that separated Jax and Naomi from the relative freedom of Salma proper. Jax figured the employees clocked in and out at the admin building, and since Jebidiah was squarely in the *nowhere* part of the Empire, security wasn't strict on who came or went into the stockyard itself. That might change after today, but that wasn't Jax's concern.

A man stood in line in front of them, a heavyset man of Earth African descent or maybe directly from Africa on Earth, given the open emigration policy currently in place for Jebidiah. He looked over his shoulder. "You got stuck playing detective, too?" The man pushed through the turnstile.

Jax looked at Naomi, then the man. "Yeah, had us inspecting up and down the line. I probably clocked six kilometers just walking along the train."

"Tell me about it," the man agreed. "I'm gonna have to soak my feet before I go to bed. Stupid assholes." He grunted, "Who robs mom and pop Co-ops just trying to get by?" Before Jax could reply, the worker waved and picked up his pace. "Damn, that's my bus!" He trotted toward a bus that had pulled up outside the gate. "Hey, wait up!" he shouted.

Jax pushed through the turnstile and watched the man vanish onto the bus. He looked around and saw Naomi exiting the stockyard. "Where to?" she asked.

He removed his gPhone from a pocket and scrolled through a few screens. He looked up, pointed down a street leading away from the stockyard. "Popular place up the street." He set off. She fell in next to him.

"I hope they have bacon," Naomi said as they approached *Bennie's Diner*.

Jax reached for the door, holding it open as Naomi entered. He looked around. Not very busy, but that was to be expected. It was still an hour or two before the lunch rush would likely happen, and the day shift crew was already at work.

A tall thin woman with gray hair held in a tight bun atop her head looked up from the counter top she was wiping down. "Hi, folks, take a seat wherever you like. I'll be right over."

Naomi smiled as she took in the scene. "Cute place. This planet just moved up a notch."

Jax slid into a booth. "Oh, from what, the bottom of the scale?"

"More or less."

The older woman arrived with a pot of coffee and two cups. The cups were a brown ceramic, polished to a high sheen. She set the cups down and filled them. "Have a chance to look at the menu?"

Naomi shook her head. "No, but if you've got bacon and eggs, I'm good."

The woman smiled. "I have just the thing." She looked at Jax. "Sweetie?"

Jax tapped his chin as he thought. "I'll have the same, but can I get hash browns?"

"Of course." She turned and left.

Naomi picked up her cup and took a sip. "This place is like one of your old-timey vids." She examined the cup. "Think they make these with the mud here?"

Jax took a sip of his coffee, then looked at the mug. "Might be where the coffee comes from, too?" He took another sip, then reached for the sugar. He said, "So, after this, we gotta get back out to the ship. Thoughts?"

Naomi looked around, then settled on a small display set into the table near the wall. It was displaying an ad for some type of medical device to help with *miner's toe,* whatever that was. She reached out and set her hand on the device. The screen immediately went blank before lines of computer code started scrolling. The now familiar blue lines began glowing along her arms and up her neck to encircle her right eye.

Jax looked around nervously but saw only the waitress back behind the counter cleaning more of the brown coffee mugs. He tried to look as casual as he could, sipping his coffee as Naomi remained motionless, pulses of blue light moving up and down her tattoos. He was taking another sip when she inhaled sharply, her hand jerking away from the device. Jax nearly spat out his coffee. The ad for the medical device resumed playing.

PET NAMES

"I think this might be their closest pass," Skip said from the ceiling. Kori and Steve were on the small bridge watching on the various displays as one of the shuttles launched from Salma made its way towards them. The number of shuttles searching the surrounding countryside had changed several times during the night and morning hours. Right now, there were only two. One was on a course that Skip projected would bring it within fifteen kilometers of their position.

The *Osprey*, being designed to sneak behind enemy lines to snoop, deliver goods or troops, or in some scenarios, attack, was not at much risk. Her active camouflage and sensor masking tech were good. The two sets of stolen ore modules, on the other hand, were another thing entirely. Steve was as confident as he could be in the camouflage rigs they'd purchased to hide the massive cargo modules, but one glitch in their wiring or failure entirely, and the passing shuttle would likely see them.

The younger of the Delphino brothers watched the screens intently. "Any indications of malfunctions from the ore modules?" he asked out loud.

"None," Rudy answered from his station. The small navigation droid was monitoring the functions of the camouflage modules remotely. So far both were active and showing no fault codes.

Kori watched out the transparent titanium window as a small dot moved into view, grew larger, but not a lot, then continued on. Skip said, "I think we're in the clear." Kori released a breath she had not realized she was holding.

Steve turned to head to the staircase and the common deck one level down. "Okay, that's good then." He consulted his gPhone. "Looks like about seven more hours before pick up." As he pocketed his phone, he said, "Hey, rollerball, Jax have a dartboard?"

"Or darts?" Kori added.

The rust-colored nav droid disengaged from his console. His squat cylinder head spun. "I think so, maybe. I'll go look." Steve nodded and headed down the stairs. Rudy zipped to the open center of the staircase and dropped.

Kori stood to follow Steve and Rudy when Skip said, "Kori, do you think he's okay?"

She looked up at the ceiling. "Jax? Yeah, of course. Why?"

There was a pause as the SI that ran the ship thought about it. Finally, it said, "Naomi is a new variable that I have been unable to quantify."

Kori smiled. "Yeah, she's definitely a variable, but I think she'll keep him safe." She rested a hand on the bulkhead. "Plus, when has Jackson Caruso ever not scraped by in a dangerous situation?"

"Good point," the SI conceded, sounding reassured to Kori's untrained ear. She headed down to the common deck.

"So..." Jax motioned to the terminal and its ad for some type of knee brace. "Success?"

Naomi shook her head. "Afraid not." She tilted her head towards the terminal device now displaying an ad for a treatment for upset stomachs. Was everyone on this planet sick from one thing or another? "Those things aren't on the planetary network. There's a server somewhere onsite that serves up the ads."

Jax nodded. "Great," he agreed. He took a bite of his hash browns. "Good." He took a few more bites. He raised a hand to flag down the waitress.

Naomi looked over her shoulder to see the older woman approaching. When the woman arrived, she said, "Need something?"

Jax smiled. "Just a question. We're thinking of getting away for the day. We just got here, though, not super familiar with the city."

The woman looked from Jax to Naomi, a twinkle in her eye. "The flats to the east are popular with young lovers." She winked. "So I hear. You can rent a skimmer at Hasim's." She held her hand out, fingers wiggling. When Jax just stared at her, she said, "Phone."

"Ah!" He handed his gPhone over. The waitress tapped on the screen a moment, then swiped a few times. She handed the device back. He looked at his phone and nodded. "Thanks!" He turned to Naomi. "Lovebug, it's not a long walk to Hasim's."

The face Naomi made was one Jax wished he could capture on his phone and attach to Naomi's contact info. She growled but recovered, smiling. "That's good news, Flat Butt."

The waitress watched the exchange, eyebrows crawling to the top of her forehead. She didn't say anything as she turned and left.

ONE MORE THING

"Steve, Kori, I think we might have an issue," Skip said over their earpieces. Steve and Kori had set up Jax's old dartboard, a relic from their first few years out of school. That was before Kori and Jax ended their relationship, when hustling visitors to Kelso at darts kept them in beer and food.

Kori threw her last dart, then said, "Oh?"

Steve added, "Wouldn't that be an *additional* issue? It's not like we don't have a few ongoing concerns right now."

There was what sounded like a sigh on the other end of the line before Skip said, "Okay, fine, we have an additional issue to worry about."

When it was clear the SI would not elaborate on his own, Kori pressed, "Which is?"

"An Imperial ship just made orbit. A—"

"What? Have they detected us?" Steve interrupted as he grabbed the darts and dart board.

Skip very clearly sighed this time. "Not that I can tell. I'm still running passives, and our stealth systems are still fully engaged. I don't think it's one of the big ones. A cutter or system patrol boat would be my guess. That said, though, getting out of here may be a bit trickier."

Steve released the breath he had been holding. "Ah, okay. Well, I guess monitor it."

"You think? I sure am glad you're here. I wouldn't have known what to do otherwise," the SI replied, then closed the channel.

Steve grimaced as he looked at Kori. "How does he put up with that? Are all droids this mouthy?"

She tightened the fabric strip that was keeping her hair back and said, "There are plenty of droids on Kelso."

Steve shrugged. "Marshall isn't a fan, so we don't interact with 'em much." He put the dart board back and handed her the darts.

The waitress came over. "Anything else?"

Jax shook his head. "No, we're done." The woman nodded and held her tablet up. She tapped a few times, then swiped towards Jax. His gPhone buzzed and he acknowledged the bill and added a generous tip.

The older woman smiled when she saw the tip. "You get some overtime?" When Jax didn't answer immediately, she pointed to his bright orange outfit, then Naomi's. "Work in the yard, right? Skimmer rental, big tip, not exactly normal for yardies." She smiled.

"Ah, yeah, sorry," Jax replied.

"Long night," Naomi added.

"I heard," the woman said. "Got the whole garrison up in arms, troopers stomping all around. Who robs little operators like that?"

Jax and Naomi exchanged a glance. He said, "Uh, what do you mean?"

Naomi added, "That's the second time someone mentioned that."

"Didn't they tell you? The scuttlebutt is that the modules that got lifted were from a handful of small mom and pop mining operations out of Abda." She tutted, "Damn shame."

Jax's cheeks started to burn. He could feel the flush creeping up. "We, uh, hadn't heard. So, you mean those lots weren't one of the larger mining corps'?"

Again, the older woman shook her head. "Not according to the rumor mill. All small operations. I'm guessing many will have to fold, sell their plots and equipment to try to recoup some of their investment." She sighed. "Tale as old as time: come out to the frontier, strike it rich. Except you're just as likely to fall victim to criminals or other settlers."

"Criminals?" Naomi asked.

The woman looked around. The diner was almost entirely empty now. The women who'd come earlier were at the opposite end, engrossed in whatever conversation they were having. "Crimson Orchid has been trying to get a leg up on the mining trade here."

"Crimson Orchid?" Jax asked.

"Some new syndicate, based on Themura, I hear." At that, both Jax and Naomi looked at each other, realization dawning on them. "Sounds like they're trying to buy up the smaller plots to get a majority on the mining board."

Jax sighed. "Because the board sets the prices, and the trade routes."

The waitress nodded. She looked over to the two women again as one waved politely. She nodded and turned to Jax and Naomi. "You two enjoy your romantic getaway. I'm sure the hubbub will be settled in a day or two."

Naomi smiled. "Yeah, probably."

When the waitress was out of earshot, Jax looked Naomi in the eyes. "Well, shit."

"Understatement of the year," she agreed.

THIRTEEN

NO TAKE BACKS

Jax and Naomi exited the diner and headed off toward Hasim's. According to the mapping app on Jax's gPhone, they had a twenty-minute walk ahead of them.

The sun was high overhead and the temperature just shy of uncomfortable. Jax wiped his brow. "How is this place so muddy and so damn hot?" He smacked the back of his neck. When he moved his hand, he looked at the dead something crushed there. "Gross."

Naomi shrugged. "Human computer hybrid experiment, not a climatologist."

Jax looked at her. "Wouldn't that be a meteorologist?"

"No, dummy. Meteorology is weather," she tutted as she kept walking.

Jax tapped his earpiece. "Skip, you all there?"

Naomi heard the call in her earpiece. "Yeah, boss. Good to hear from you. Everything okay?"

Before Jax could answer, Rudy added, "Good to hear your voice."

Jax smiled. "Back at ya, buddy. Everything okay there?"

Kori answered. She sounded winded. "Oh, you know,

killing time. We found your old dart board. I can't believe you kept that thing!"

Naomi looked at Jax as they waited at a crosswalk. Most of the ground and hover cars were older models, likely exported from the core shortly after the war settled down.

Jax smiled. "Memento. Anyway, listen, I think we have a problem." He looked up and down the street. No other pedestrians nearby. "I think we got played. I think we stole that ore from a bunch of small operations, as part of a plan to pressure them to sell to a syndicate."

Steve said, "What? How?"

"Come again?" Kori added.

Naomi answered, "We found a source for local gossip. She was pretty sure."

"Well, damn," Kori said.

"What now?" Rudy asked.

Before Jax could answer, Skip cut back in, "Oh, before you answer, we picked up an Imperial ship in orbit. Not a big one, but probably should factor into whatever plan you're cooking up, boss."

Jax groaned, "Great." The light changed and he and Naomi crossed the street. They were entering what must be part of Salma's luxury shopping district. Several store fronts were advertising high end clothing and home goods. "Obviously, we can't let our client have the ore."

"Obviously?" Steve repeated. "They paid us. We did the job. I get you're not thrilled that he lied to you and all, but what's the problem? We have a timetable. Kori needs to get back to work, and Marshall will be waiting for me. Plus, we barely pulled off stealing this stuff once. Now you wanna, what? Put it back?"

Over the line, the sound of Steve yelping came through loud and clear. Kori said, "So, what's the plan? The client's representatives will be here in..." She trailed off, likely looking at the time display on her gPhone. "Seven hours. Just past sundown."

Jax looked in a store as they passed. It was a technology store: latest model gPhones and tablets, home security rigs, and more. "I'll think of something. Just keep your eyes and sensors open. Now that we know who we're dealing with, assume simply paying us and being on their way isn't the plan. I'm guessing it's either a setup, or we're not supposed to survive the pickup."

Steve and Kori looked at each other, then turned, making slow turns, taking in their current setting. The valley that up until then had seemed like an excellent place to avoid detection now looked like a great place to ambush the crew of the *Osprey*. Kori tapped her earpiece. "Baxter, you heard all that?"

"Of course," the combat droid replied.

"I'm thinking it might not be a bad idea if you patrolled the area a bit more. I'm looking at these valley walls and thinking we're in a distinctly high-ground-free situation."

"Agreed." The channel closed.

NICE AFTERNOON STROLL

Jax looked at the technology store again and turned to Naomi. "I have an idea, kind of."

She raised an eyebrow. "It's kind of an idea?"

He shrugged. "I guess, to be clear, it's definitely part of an idea. Whether it's good or bad hasn't been determined."

"But we're about to determine, aren't we?"

He pressed the button to open the sliding doors. "You wanted a partnership." He grinned and walked in.

The store was not very busy, but it wasn't empty. The lone salesman was helping a moderately well-dressed couple. He looked up. "I'll be right with you folks." He smiled and turned his attention back to the couple. "Where was I? Oh, so you'll definitely want the BFG-9000 on an auto tracking base, somewhere kind of central to your property and main gate. You'll get the most protection out of a single unit that way."

Jax guided Naomi to a wall of tablets. She looked at the display. "Need a new tablet?"

He shook his head. "No. Think you can do your," he

held up a hand, fingers wiggling, "thing on these to make a call to the Imperial garrison?"

"You want to call in the Imperials?" Both of her eyes looked like they might pop out of her head. "Determination made. This is a bad idea."

Jax just stared at her, then said, "Got a better one?"

She was silent as she looked at the wall of tablets. She looked at Jax out of the corner of her eye. "Nope. Cover me." He turned slightly to keep an eye on the salesman. Naomi picked one of the lowest cost tablets. "Crappier firmware and likely no firewall. It's always those with the least who get screwed." She mumbled as she gingerly examined the device. She wrapped both hands around the sides of the device. Immediately her arms began to glow their now familiar blue from fingertip to wrist. She had rolled down the sleeves of her jumpsuit to help keep the glowing tattoos from attracting attention. The tablet's screen came to life, first the graphical user interface, then a black screen with lines of code. She looked at Jax. Reaching up, she tapped his earpiece.

"Hello?" Jax heard over the line. It wasn't any of his friends back at the *Osprey*. He looked at Naomi. She made a *hurry up* motion.

"Uh, hi. I've got information on the stolen ore modules."

"Sir, this line is for emergency use only," the bored sounding Imperial said.

"Asshole, are you listening?" Jax ground out. "I said I know where the stolen ore is and who stole it."

"Sir, if you don't show a little more respect, I'll have to dispatch shock troopers."

Jax sighed and rubbed his face. "Look, man. The ore modules are sitting a dozen or so kilometers outside town. Want to know where or not?"

"Please hold." Before Jax could respond, the bored sounding man was replaced with an inane instrumental version of a song that was popular a year or two ago.

Without warning, the line went dead. Jax looked around to see Naomi placing the tablet back on its display shelf. The couple who had been with the salesman were exiting the store. The salesman was approaching. Rubbing his hands together, he said, "Hi folks, sorry for the wait. What can I help you with?" He looked at the wall of tablets. "Looking to upgrade or...?"

Jax turned, smiling. "Oh, sorry, no. We're just window shopping." As if to further explain, he subtly gestured to his jumpsuit, then Naomi's.

The man's face fell. His reply was frosty. "I see. Well, please try not to touch everything. I have to clean it all before closing." He turned and walked away.

"Rude," Naomi whispered. Jax nodded. She looked at him. "Didn't sound like it went well."

He shook his head. "No, we'll have to try again." He looked at the salesman, who was not at all subtly watching them. "Somewhere else." He headed for the door, Naomi in tow.

COMPANY IS COMING

"We have company," Baxter said over the shared comm channel.

Kori and Steve were on the small bridge with Rudy. They looked at each other, then at a display showing Baxter's relative position to the *Osprey*. Kori said, "What's up?" To keep their power signature hard to spot, Skip had turned off the environmental regulator. It was hot aboard the small ship. Kori's skin glistened a deep ebony. She looked at her phone. Still five hours from the scheduled meet with the client.

"I'm picking up two, what looks like, troop transports," the combat droid replied.

"Imperial?" Steve asked, his own much paler skin glistening with sweat.

"Impossible to say yet, but I don't think so. Sending visual data to Skip. He might be able to run it through the recognition database."

"On it," the ship's SI replied. Less than a minute later, he added, "Yeah, probably not Imperial. Looks like older models, maybe a year or two post-war."

"So probably our friends," Kori surmised.

"As good a guess any," Baxter replied. "What do you want me to do?"

Kori looked at the terrain display again, seeing where Baxter was. Skip had updated it to show the current vector of the two transports. "Keep patrolling and mark where those transports land. Stay out of sight."

"Copy." The channel closed.

Steve looked at the woman next to him, his brow beaded with sweat. He tapped his earpiece, "Jax?"

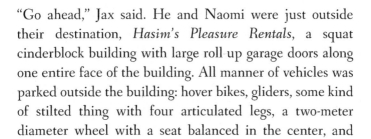

"Go ahead," Jax said. He and Naomi were just outside their destination, *Hasim's Pleasure Rentals*, a squat cinderblock building with large roll up garage doors along one entire face of the building. All manner of vehicles was parked outside the building: hover bikes, gliders, some kind of stilted thing with four articulated legs, a two-meter diameter wheel with a seat balanced in the center, and more.

"I think our client is getting set up for whatever bad things they have planned for us."

"Shit, okay. We'll be there shortly. I think."

"You think?" Steve asked.

"See you soon," Jax tapped his earpiece, closing the channel. He looked around. "Still no better ideas?"

Naomi exhaled. "Nope. As much as I wish that weren't the case."

Jax hunched his shoulders. "Here we go, then." He walked across the street toward Hasim's. Naomi followed, watching as a delivery van backed up to the side of a convenience store down the block. The hover truck rocked slightly as it moved. It made a pitiful sounding beeping as it reversed.

A heavyset man with skin nearly the same shade of brown as the coffee mugs at the diner walked out of a small office. "Can I help you two?"

Naomi put on a smile as she clutched Jax's hand. "Hi! We're looking to rent two skimmers?" She added some uncertainty to her voice.

The man eyed them both up and down suspiciously. Jax was about to try to add to the story, when the man, presumably Hasim, clapped his hands. "Wonderful! I was worried that with all the hullabaloo going on at the stockyard, opening today would be a waste." He smiled broadly. Jax exchanged a look with Naomi, then shrugged. "Come, friends! Let's get you set up with your rentals!" He turned to head back into the building. "Where are you two thinking of heading? The plains? Lover's overlook?" He waggled a finger. "There is a cleaning deposit."

Naomi pantomimed a vomiting motion.

They followed the rotund man into the building. As they entered, Naomi slowed down and ran a hand along one of the four-limbed walker vehicles. Her arm glowed blue as she interfaced with the device. She repeated the motion on a three-wheeled vehicle, likely designed for getting around the city on.

Hasim sat down behind a desk covered in papers and tablets. He pushed tablets out of his way. He gestured. "Sit, sit, this won't take long. You'll soon be airborne and on your way." He craned his neck to look back outside. "Looks like the weather plans to Co-operate."

Naomi gently moved a pile of what looked like rental slips and invoices from the seat to the floor, then sat down.

Hasim opened his mouth to say something but was cut

off by a clatter from the showroom area where one of his rentals appeared to be going berserk. He looked at his two customers, then the commotion. "I will be right back!" He leapt from his chair faster than Jax would have thought a man his size could move. Several expletives in a language Jax did not recognize came from the showroom area. The three-wheeled vehicle leapt from the garage area to collide with the delivery vehicle that was servicing the convenience store. The driver immediately began shouting and waving Hasim over.

The poor man looked at his three-wheeler, then at the stilted walker as it crushed a trash receptacle on the street corner before harassing a bus full of people.

Naomi watched the action, then stood up. "Let's go. I told that walker thing to stomp around, then head off down the street doing as much damage as it can. If it's not stuck, three-wheeler is gonna take off in the opposite direction shortly." They exited the office slowly, looking for any sign of Hasim. He was already near the street, trying to corral the wayward walker.

LET'S GO

Jax and Naomi crept around the back of the single-story building. They could still hear Hasim shouting. Out back, they found a row of sleek winged craft parked in a row. They were all garishly painted with neon colors in stripes and zigzags. Each skimmer featured a cockpit in which the pilot lay prone, surrounded by a transparent shell. All the skimmers' cockpits were open, like clamshells. The main fuselage of the sleek craft featured a swept-back wing design with articulated turbo fans set in each wide wing. A small grav-lift was embedded in the lower section of the body to assist in maneuvering.

Jax looked the lightweight vehicles over. He turned to Naomi. "Think you can fly one?"

She shrugged. "Only one way to find out. There must be an RI installed or something." She gestured to the nimble-looking craft. "They can't let any yahoo with no piloting skills climb into these willy-nilly." She looked at the nearest craft. "Can they?"

Jax quirked an eyebrow. "Any yahoo, huh?" She made a rude gesture, then turned to a different skimmer, a bright purple one. As she got situated on the foam platform, the two halves of the cockpit closed. The entire assembly slid back toward the main body of the fuselage.

From somewhere inside the cockpit with her, a voice said, "Hello, I am your flight assistant. There are many available options, depending on your skill level."

Naomi cut the basic intelligence off. "I'm not a pilot. I need all the help you can give." She reached out to touch the main console, her hand glowing.

Jax approached one of the open cockpits and crawled in. Once situated and comfortable on the foam platform, he found the canopy control. As the two transparent halves closed, the entire cockpit slid backwards into the body of the skimmer. The fuselage unfolded as the craft powered up, wings hinging down to lock into position. He looked over at Naomi and gave a thumbs up. She returned the gesture.

As Jax taxied his skimmer away from the others, a voice said, "Hello, I am your flight assistant. Would you like me to handle take off?"

Jax shook his head. "Nope. Disable all flight assistance."

"Very well. You need only say, '*flight assist*,' to re-engage my services."

He pushed the throttle all the way forward. The powerful turbofans roared as the skimmer leapt into the air.

From her skimmer, Naomi watched Jax soar into the air. She looked to the side just in time to see Hasim jogging towards her, a tablet in one hand. She quickly reached out and touched the primary control module again, accessing its primitive systems, disabling the remote kill switch. "Get us airborne and fly," she said out loud.

"Very well," the RI replied.

She concentrated on the control systems of her skimmer, finding the software controls for the wireless networking gear.

"Hey, what the hell?" Jax exclaimed over their comm channel. Ahead, his skimmer was banking in a wide arc back towards the rental facility.

Naomi closed her eyes. Her tattoos glowed brightly, all of them. Using the networking gear in her own skimmer, she reached out to Jax's. It was easy to disable the recall functions and then enable a rudimentary firewall. It would not keep a determined hacker out, but would most definitely keep Hasim out long enough. "You're good," she said out loud.

"Thanks." His skimmer circled back to be alongside hers. "I didn't know your tattoo magic worked long distance."

She sighed, "It doesn't. But my skimmer and yours are on the same network, so I...well. It's not fun or easy. We're good now. I threw up some simple firewalls."

"Fair enough. Thanks." He waggled his skimmer's wings, then shot off ahead of her.

The sun was low in the sky now.

PART FOUR

FOURTEEN

"I've got two, no, three ships on sensors," Skip reported. Kori and Steve were in the common area looking over the terrain details Baxter had been sending. The ship's SI added, "Looks like about ten minutes out."

Kori looked at the ceiling. "How far are Jax and Naomi?"

"Maybe fifteen, twenty at the most. Their skimmers don't have very sophisticated computers. They're not on my passive scopes yet."

Steve looked at the ceiling. "And those transports?"

Baxter answered, "They made their drops and headed out. Both are parked about two kilometers from the back of this valley. I've got eyes on one of the strike teams. The other was moving west when I lost visual. Both teams are well armed."

Skip added, "I was able to pick them up, sporadically." The main entertainment screen updated with an aerial rendering of the valley and surrounding terrain out to five kilometers. The two transports were red squares. The two attack teams were red rectangles. The inbound craft were red circles. The *Osprey* was a green circle. Baxter was a green triangle.

"Lot of red," Steve observed.

"Yeah, but they don't have a me," the combat droid huffed, certain of his abilities.

"Let's hope," Kori said.

"Jax, Naomi, we've got inbound," Skip said over the shared comm channel.

"Sit rep?" Jax asked.

"Kori and Steve are prepping now in the armory. Baxter is on walk about. The two strike teams are in place. Baxter is shadowing one of them. I've got the other on tactical, but we don't have weapons on them."

"Copy that." He consulted the small computer display in front of him. "These things have pretty shitty nav software, but I think we're about fifteen out. They're fast, but not that fast."

"The inbounds will be skids down in just under ten," the ship's SI replied.

Jax pushed the throttle on his skimmer all the way to the stops. Several indicators lit up. On the small display, a warning appeared showing that prolonged use of the throttle at full power may damage the craft and cause forfeiture of any security deposit. Jax saw Naomi's skimmer follow suit, keeping pace with his own.

From her skimmer, Naomi asked, "So, is there a plan for when we get there?"

Jax smiled to himself. "I'm sure something will come to one of us."

Naomi groaned and reached out to the small console in

front of her, tattoos glowing around her face and hand. The small display in front of her blinked, then went to the familiar scrolling-code mode.

"The lead freighter is hailing us," Skip announced.

Kori and Steve had moved to the bridge for a better view of the situation. Kori smoothed her hair back, tightening the piece of cloth that held it in place. She looked at the communications screen mounted from the ceiling and nodded.

The screen came to life, filled with the face of a stern woman of Asian descent. "We are here for our goods."

"Hello to you, too." Kori smiled. "We're finalizing a few things, if you can give us a few minutes?"

"We'll be landing in two minutes. Our representative will meet you at the nearest set of modules to your ship." The screen went black.

Steve looked at her. "That went well."

She shrugged. "Well, we already know they're planning to kill us, so ..." She looked at the ceiling. "Baxter, get ready."

"Always am," the combat droid replied.

The two humans headed for the staircase. Kori stopped at Rudy's station. "Keep Jax and Naomi informed."

The droid's head made a full rotation, his optic sensors spinning. "Will do. Be careful." Kori patted the small droid on the head as she passed.

As Steve and Kori exited the *Osprey,* Kori pointed past the mouth of the small valley they'd parked in. "There." In the distance, two heavy lift freighters were rumbling their way to the ground, their powerful lift engines churning up a minor dust storm. The third was hovering over them in an over watch position.

"Reassuring," Steve murmured, nodding toward the hovering vessel. A hatch on the nearest ship opened and three people emerged. Kori and Steve walked toward the trio, stopping at the agreed upon ore module.

"Hi." Steve waved as the trio arrived.

"Hello," the lead man said, bowing. He looked at the large ore modules. "You were successful." He looked Steve up and down. "But you are not Jackson Caruso." The other two, a man and a woman in crisp black suits, were staring at Kori and Steve, sizing them up. Kori noticed that the woman was the same one from their earlier conversation. Above the neck of each of their immaculately tailored suits were the barest hints of tattoos.

Kori took point. "You're right. Jax... Jackson is unavailable at the moment. He asked us to welcome you. He'll be along shortly." She gestured to the set of ore modules nearest them and the one a hundred or so meters away, closer to the two freighters. "As you can see, we've retrieved the two train cars' worth of ore, as agreed."

The leader of the trio nodded to his associates. One moved to the nearest set of modules, the other headed toward the further set. "And our specified lots are accounted for?"

Steve and Kori nodded. This time Steve answered, "Yes, sir. You'll find the designated lots in each set of modules."

The man bowed his head, "Excellent work." He looked past Kori and Steve toward the not too distant walls of the valley. Knowing what to look for, Kori spotted the smallest grin form on his lips. He turned and looked first at the nearer of his associates, the woman, who had a handheld scanner in her hand. She nodded. The third of their group had a similar scanner and nodded his confirmation. The leader of the group nodded, then removed his gPhone from his pocket. He smiled at Steve and Kori. "Thank you." He looked down at his phone, thumb poised over something on the screen. Over his shoulder, Kori saw his two associates remove pistols from inside their suit jackets. From recessed panels on the hovering freighter, two blaster turrets emerged.

His thumb twitched toward the gPhone only to explode in a red mist.

...NOT THE PLAYER

Baxter, they're down with the bad guys now. Are you ready? Skip wirelessly beamed to his companion hiding in the scrub brush behind a group of almost a dozen armed men and women.

I'm ready, the combat droid beamed back as his forearms shifted to allow half meter long blades to deploy. They clacked as the individual segments locked into place. Once locked into place, energy flowed into them causing them to glow crimson. Quieter than a mechanical being his size should be able to be, he crept up to within two meters of the nearest enemies.

"Hello, I am here to kill you," he said, loud enough for the nearest woman to hear before he leapt into the middle of their formation, blades cutting through the light armor they wore like it wasn't there.

When he was sure that each target was dead and that his attack hadn't attracted the attention of the team on the opposite side of the valley, he powered down the blades. In all, he'd killed the entire strike team without a single sound making it to the team across the valley floor hearing. As he moved toward the edge of the valley wall, his dual shoulder railguns deployed, as did his forearm blasters. He sighted on the man talking to Steve and Kori.

As he watched the exchange, he saw the man working his phone, thumb ready to activate something. With no better intel to operate from, the combat droid made a decision. He fired a single shot. The sound of the shot came after the man's hand and gPhone exploded in a red mist.

Steve and Kori were nearly to the ground before the Asian man with now only one hand, realized what was happening, just before the loud crack echoed through the valley. Baxter's railguns.

By the time they hit the ground and shimmied toward a rock barely big enough to provide cover, the wounded man had darted back to the relative safety of his nearest colleague.

Blaster fire erupted from the opposite wall of the valley, chewing up the ground around Steve and Kori's small boulder. Rock chips and damp soil pelted them.

Steve glanced over his shoulder as energy bolts lanced from one side of the valley wall to the other, Baxter. The weapons fire pinning them down abated as the second team of attackers changed targets to the valley wall opposite them. Shouts echoed down into the valley from above.

The freighter opened fire as well, its more powerful energy weapons igniting the grass around the two defenders.

Steve looked at Kori as she ducked behind their meager cover. "We gotta find someplace less exposed!" She nodded.

"Incoming!" was shouted over their shared comm channel, causing Kori to flinch. In the distance, two small craft zipped in alongside the hovering freighter before diving steeply to make a semi-controlled crash landing. The confusion caused by the two inbound skimmers was enough to give Kori and Steve a chance to sprint toward the *Osprey*. They made it as far as the far side of the ore module before the hovering freighter resumed its firing.

The two remaining intact members of the initial trio turned their attention to the skimmers, now sitting in deep furrows. Jax and Naomi had ejected just before impact and were crouched next to one of the landed freighters in the shadow of its landing gear.

"Weapons would be nice," Jax groaned, rubbing his elbow. His jumpsuit had a rip along one arm, and blood was seeping from a cut below his shoulder.

Naomi looked at him and winked. She placed both hands on the hull of the old freighter. Her hands and face lit up. "Damnit," she hissed.

"What?"

She moved her hands to different parts of the landing gear and hull plating. "Haven't found any live circuits yet. Wait! There," she said, eyes closed. Jax watched impatiently until the same recessed weapons as those on the hovering freighter deployed and took aim at the other landed freighter. She only got a few shots off before Jax pushed her to the ground. The man and woman that had been inspecting the ruins of the skimmers had taken aim at them.

The battle near the top of the valley dwindled, leaving both sections of the valley wall smoking and aflame. Large blackened impact craters dotted both sides.

Kori and Steve charged out from behind the nearest ore

module, blasters blazing. The large man fell to the ground, his shoulder a smoking ruin. The woman turned to engage the armed threats but only fired a few shots, enough to cause her two assailants to drop for cover. She darted to the freighter Naomi was firing on, running up the boarding ramp.

Jax looked up and ushered Naomi out from under the freighter they were using for cover as its lift engines powered up. Whoever was at the controls was in a hurry as the freighter began to rise before the engines were even at full power. Naomi and Jax were blown to the ground by the powerful energy exhaust. Jax screamed as he was rolled several feet, striking his bloodied elbow on a rock.

From his position on the ground, he saw Kori and Steve get up and move toward the two men they'd incapacitated. At the same time, he saw the *Osprey* lift off the ground, the small missile launcher ports open on her sides. Two of the small, highly explosive missiles leapt from their housing and crossed the distance between the *Osprey* and the hovering freighter in seconds, exploding against its side. The much larger ship lurched to the side, brought its blasters to bear, and opened fire on the smaller Valerian Co-op Infiltrator. The *Osprey* tilted and increased altitude as it unleashed another pair of missiles.

"Those things aren't cheap," he whispered to himself as the freighter that was hovering over the battle listed to port, then slammed to the ground, gouging a furrow nearly fifty meters long in the soggy valley floor.

The freighter that the woman had boarded moments ago, heedless of anything or anyone around it, engaged its sub-light engines. The powerful thrust struck the other freighter, the one Jax and Naomi had been hiding under, forcing it almost back to the ground. One of the landing legs, the one Naomi had touched to hack into the ship's systems, hit the ground and bent. It would not be retracting into the hull any time soon.

UNLIKELY BACKUP

As the least damaged freighter climbed, its sister ship, the one it had pushed to the ground earlier, did, as well, albeit much slower. Jax watched as the *Osprey* moved to get clear of the valley walls as it lobbed two more missiles at the nearest freighter. Explosions rocked the ship but didn't bring it down. The ship returned fire with its blasters, raking the hull of the much smaller ship. Until the *Osprey* could get above the other ships, she was limited to missiles. The most powerful weapon the infiltrator had, the particle beam cannon, was mounted on the underside of the ship.

"Hi!" Kori said as she and Steve reached Jax and Naomi's position, their prisoners in tow.

The one-handed man growled when he saw Jax. "You will suffer greatly for this betrayal."

In the distance, the sound of engines, lots of them, was building. Ships were inbound.

Jax looked at the man, his face serious. "Look, I don't care what you flower power assholes get up to out here on the Edge, but you came to me, at my home, and lied to me." He stepped right up to the man, their chests an inch apart.

"Your boss tricked me into robbing mom and pop operations. Independent operations. That hurts me," he pushed the man away and tapped his chest, "in a special place." He leaned in so that his face was inches from the other man. "Oh, and then you all were going to kill us." He stood and turned away from the man.

Jax looked off in the distance at the approaching ships, now very visible, and very Imperial. He looked to the one-handed man, then to his friend. The second man's shoulder was a blackened mess of burnt fabric and skin. "I'd give you a message for your boss, but well, I don't think you'll be seeing him anytime soon."

The more damaged freighter, likely seeing it had nowhere to run, turned, bringing its weapons to bear on the small party standing next to the ore module. Steve and Kori registered the danger a split second before Jax and Naomi. Jax was about to swear, when a powerful railgun round struck the already damaged freighter. Another, then another, then a fourth round struck the ship. Pieces of the damaged vessel rained down on the valley floor. One of the blaster turrets that a moment ago was about to vaporize Jax and his friends crumpled inward and exploded.

Jax saw the smile that had formed on both prisoner's faces fade as they realized they would almost certainly be arrested, alive.

The Imperial ships roared overhead: three assault shuttles, a full wing of victory class starfighters, and a troop transport.

The starfighters moved to surround the fleeing freighter. It opened fire, destroying one of the nimble fighters. The remaining five opened fire, quickly destroying the weapons systems, then engines, driving the freighter to the ground, where it landed in a crumpled metal heap. The troop transport landed a few hundred meters from Jax and the others. He looked at his friends, making a motion that caused Kori and Steve to toss their pistols to the ground.

The side of the transport opened as the heavy assault shuttles circled over the other two freighters. Twelve shock troops filed out, followed by a young man in a crisp crimson officer's uniform. Jax and the others remained where they were, waiting for the approaching entourage.

Once the immediate threat of the fleeing freighter was handled, the fighters moved to encircle the *Osprey*. Jax watched as the ship gently sat back down on the dirt two hundred or so meters away. Rudy or Skip—both, likely—were playing nice. That was good. Jax hoped that Baxter would remain hidden until this was over. There was already a lot to try to explain. A combat droid with heavy ordinance was not something he wanted to add to the list.

The troopers moved to surround the small group, their blaster carbines held at the ready. Naomi looked at Jax, who shrugged.

The officer arrived. Jax figured the haughty-looking officer couldn't be much older than him. "Which one of you is in charge?"

Jax slowly raised his hand. "I guess that would be me. I'm Jackson Caruso." He hitched his thumb over his shoulder, toward the *Osprey*. "Captain of the independent transport *Osprey*."

FIFTEEN

FIELD TRIP

The young officer eyed Jax appraisingly, then looked at one of the shock troopers. "Take them all into custody."

Before anyone could raise their voice to protest, the ring of shock troopers collapsed on them. Rough, armored hands grabbed them, forcing their wrists into binders. The one-handed man tried to fight back and was rendered unconscious by the butt of an Imperial blaster carbine.

The officer removed a standard issue gPhone from his pocket. "Alert the brig. We're sending up visitors." He turned to Jax. "Who is aboard your ship?"

Jax straightened. "Droids... sir. If we're going to be interrogated, may I ask that my ship be allowed to remain here on the planet? I can instruct the ship's computer to upload the data you'll want to check out."

The man gave it some thought. "That will be fine, at least for now. I'll leave a team here to watch over it." He didn't wait for Jax to say thank you or anything else. He turned and walked back to his transport. The troopers nudged everyone to fall in behind the officer.

The ride up to the Imperial patrol ship in orbit was silent. Kori had tried to get Jax and Naomi to talk about their time in Salma, but a trooper had stalked over, and with the help of his weapon, demanded silence. Twenty minutes later, the transport glided into the docking bay of the Imperial light cruiser and docked with a thunk.

As they walked through the hangar, Jax looked around. This ship was considerably smaller than the ship they'd recently been on and the one he had fled. The docking bay was still massive compared to the *Osprey*.

The port and starboard bulkheads of the cavernous space were adorned with banners for campaigns the ship had fought in and fighter squadrons based aboard it. Near the hatch they were heading for, he saw a banner with the stylized body of Zeus lying defeated at the feet of an anonymous, featureless warrior. The campaign banner of the last battle in the Unification War, the Battle of Zeus. The battle his parents had died hoping to avoid. The fleet they'd helped escape was meant to evacuate the Independent Planets Governing council. They were too slow. The battle on the surface lasted only slightly longer than the battle in orbit had. It was the end of the Independents; their fleet had been broken and scattered, their governing council eliminated. The surrender came less than a week after the Battle of Zeus.

When they arrived at the brig, the two gangsters were given one cell, and the crew of the *Osprey* went into a neighboring cell. A medic came in to tend to the one-handed man's stump. The entire time he was being treated, he glared at Jax.

A junior officer walked in to the brig, tablet in hand.

She looked down at it, then at the two groups in the cells. "Captain Caruso?" Jax stood up. She smiled. She could not have been more than a year or two out of the academy. "The captain would like to see you." She gestured to the trooper standing guard near the main hatch. The gray armored trooper opened the cell and stood back for Jax to exit, closing the door quickly behind him, lest any of his friends try to escape, or something.

The junior officer, who didn't say anything to Jax during their walk from the brig to an interrogation room, closed the door behind Jax as he walked in. The room was plain, a rectangular table in the center, two chairs on either side. A camera was mounted in the corner near the ceiling, opposite the door.

He sat down facing the door. Thoughts of his parents drifted into his mind.

The Unification Wars had ended twenty years ago. Jax was five when the Independents surrendered. There weren't very many left at that point. His parents were both upper level commanders. Both were dead. All the Independents' senior leadership was, in fact, dead.

Thomas and Alison had been Indies from the moment the movement started, largely because of Thomas' mother, Lucy. She was a founding member of the Co-op that had built Kelso Station and had been what Thomas had always jokingly referred to as a "space libertarian." He wasn't far off, and despite the joking, the apple hadn't fallen far from the tree.

Captain Thomas Caruso had captained the Independent cruiser *Washington* from the moment the ship had sailed out of the Apollo Shipyards in orbit over Zeus to the moment she rammed the Imperial battlecruiser that was ripping the fleet he was leading to shreds. His sacrifice had allowed the remaining ships to get clear and escape.

Admiral Alison Caruso had commanded the Indie fleet first from the orbital command center over Zeus, then, after that facility was destroyed, from the flagship of the ragtag fleet, the *Washington,* until she rammed the Imperials, taking both Carusos with her.

The door to the interrogation room opened.

COMING KINDA CLEAN

A man in an impeccable Imperial Navy uniform walked in. He had a riding crop under one arm. His black hair was cut high and tight, not a strand out of place, and Jax guessed it was kept at regulation length daily.

"Is that a riding crop? Like for riding horses?" Jax asked as the man came to stand across the table from him. The captain placed the crop on the table, its shiny metal topper, the emblem of the Empire, clinking against the acrylic table.

"You're Jackson—Jax—Caruso. Son of Thomas and Alison." Neither were questions. "Your family founded independent station Kelso," he added.

Jax looked up. "I mean, Memaw was one of the founders, but it's not like it's our family space station or anything. You know the answer to the rest." He smiled politely.

"You don't like the Empire very much, do you?"

Jax made a show of looking around the room. "What's not to like? I mean, my friends and I stopped a massive theft that occurred right under your nose, and your lackey hauled us up here, threw us in the brig." He frowned. "And that's just today." He locked his eyes with the captain. "What's not to like about the Empire?"

The man stared, unblinking, then slid the chair in front of him out, taking a seat opposite Jax. "Quite the mouth you have." He held up a hand to cut off whatever Jax was about to say. "I knew your parents." Jax closed his mouth. "There's no reason you'd have known that, of course. We crossed paths a few times in the old days."

"Before you sold out the alliance, you mean," Jax growled, the heat of old rage building inside him. "Or were the old days when your ship was firing on Apollo station?"

The captain, the tag on his uniform read *Hollister*, nodded slowly, silently. "What were you and your friends doing on Jebidiah? How do I know you weren't involved in the ore theft?" He tilted his head as if he were examining an interesting specimen under a microscope. "Isn't it possible you and your friends are the thieves, and you've simply changed your story to try to avoid a penal colony?"

Jax ignored the hypothetical. "What are you planning to do with us?" When Captain Hollister didn't answer, Jax added, "How about a trade, a little tit for tat? Quid—"

"Yes, I get it," Hollister interrupted. "To answer your first question, I haven't decided. If you were involved, you'll be prosecuted. If you tell me everything you know, if your story is true, and those other men are in fact Crimson Orchid? Well, that would be quite the boon to my career, and I'd be very appreciative." He grinned. The grin didn't reach his eyes. The smile faded as quickly as it appeared. "Your turn."

Jax put a lid on his anger. "Those two men. They are Crimson Orchid. They work for a man called Ichiko. I never got his first name. We dropped him off on Themura before coming here." He saw the expression of barely contained glee spreading across the other man's face. "Those two men and their three freighters were supposed to pick up the ore and make off with it."

The captain absently drummed his fingers on the table. "And what were you doing there?" He reached out and rubbed the end of his riding crop.

Jax slowly moved his head from side to side. "Well..."

The captain waved his free hand. "Let's not beat around the bush, Captain Caruso. You and your people, if I had to guess, are the ones who stole the ore. Your ship has the power to lift those modules. It was parked right next to them, in fact. Then you, what? Reconsidered?" He tilted his head. "It was you, after all, that called the garrison, I assume? Then called my ship directly?"

Jax was silent as it occurred to him that the Imperials had not intervened by chance. Naomi had contacted them somehow. He nodded. "Yeah, we were tricked into the job, and when we found out who we'd impacted, we decided to change the deal." He intentionally left out that fact that the Crimson Orchid had planned to kill them all and likely frame them.

"If what you say is true, that these men and their ships are Crimson Orchid, you made a bold choice. They've been growing quite powerful out here on the Edge. You've likely made a powerful enemy."

Jax shrugged. "Right is right."

The Imperial man pursed his lips. "Indeed." He stood, and Jax stood with him. "I'll be back." He rapped once on the door with his riding crop. The door slid open, and he left.

"Can I get a snack while I wait?" Jax shouted.

TRUTH AND CONSEQUENCES

"You could have led with your ability to override Imperial computer systems," Kori said. An officious lieutenant had moved them to a conference room. The officer didn't offer any explanation and only stared down the two Crimson Orchid men, who demanded to be released. The conference room was considerably nicer than their cell, but the guard outside the door, and the *locked* icon on the control panel, made it clear they were not yet free to go.

Naomi was sitting at the terminal set in the tabletop. It had been locked down remotely—which was next to useless against Naomi's gifts. Both of her arms glowed brightly. Her eyes were closed, outlined in pulsing blue. "Jax is in one of the interrogation rooms," she said, ignoring the other woman's observation.

"Kinda cool," Steve said. He reached down to poke Naomi's forearm. Kori swatted his hand away.

"Shut up. Both of you," Naomi said. "Captain...Hollister, I guess, is with the two goons now." She was silent.

"What—" Steve started but stopped when Naomi looked up, glaring at him.

Kori had moved to pacing the length of the room. "Okay, so what now?" She turned to Naomi. "Can you do some...whatever this is," she gestured to the other woman's glowing arms, "to get them to release us?"

Naomi thought for a minute, her hands never leaving the terminal. "Maybe." She turned her full attention back to the small terminal.

As she worked, Steve munched on one of the veggie wraps a steward had left them. "These are good." He held one out to Kori.

"I can't believe we got stuck with this," the shock trooper said to his companion. He gestured to the Valerian Co-op Infiltrator sitting dark and powered down on the ground a hundred meters away. The boarding ramp was down, but they'd been ordered to not board the vessel unless necessary.

The other trooper nodded. "Yeah, I think it's because I pissed off the Lieutenant."

"What'd you do this time?" The first trooper resumed walking the path they'd worn in the scrub grass.

"I was late to muster this morning. I was with Stacy."

"The gunnery officer?"

"No, that's Linda. She broke it off. Stacy is the engineering second watch lead."

"Can't you keep it in your pants until you're off duty?"

His friend shrugged. "Technically, I was off duty when we got together." The other trooper sighed.

They looked off toward one of the Crimson Orchid freighters. Scanner crews and shock troopers were all over the hull, coming and going through a large hole in the side of the ship. Temporary cages held the surviving crews off to the side. The unruly freighter crews had started their captivity shouting all manner of obscenities. They'd gotten bored with that fairly quickly and were all sitting against the cage bars talking now.

The two troopers continued away from the *Osprey* along the patrol route they had been walking since their forces had left the planet. Crouched next to a piece of the valley wall that had fallen to the floor in the earlier fighting, Baxter watched. Thus far, he'd remained undetected and had spent his time watching the patrols and snooping on their comms.

Baxter stood and crept toward the *Osprey*. He had been careful not to establish contact with the ship wirelessly in case the Imperials had monitoring equipment.

Jax was sitting in the interrogation room, eating a hamburger, when the captain returned, riding crop in hand. The hatch closed behind him as he said, "Enjoying?"

Jax took a bite and nodded. "Willy gud," he said around the mouthful. He chewed and swallowed. "So? What's the verdict?"

The captain sat down across from him. "They haven't talked." He held up a hand when Jax opened his mouth. "But we have the survivors from the crews of the freighters. The Crimson Orchid apparently paid them far less than the two men we have." He rapped the metal end of his crop against the table. "I have to take some of your story at face value as those freighter crews don't know anything about you, your friends, or your ship. They were hired to grab those modules."

Jax smiled. "So we can go?"

The captain was tapping his chin, debating Jax's fate, when the door to the interrogation room slid open to reveal a young ensign. "I'm sorry to interrupt, sir. We've received orders." The young woman offered a tablet.

The captain leaned back and snatched it from her hand, examining it. Jax craned his neck to see the screen. The other man noticed and turned enough to keep the screen hidden. He handed the tablet back and said, "Escort him and his friends to a shuttle and get them planet-side and recall our forces immediately." He turned to Jax. "To answer your question, yes, you're free to go. We've got somewhere to be, so I'll have to continue my investigation en route. If I have questions, I know where to find you." He smirked, then stood and strode out of the room, leaving the young ensign to stare at Jax.

Jax looked up at the ensign. "I'm ready whenever you are."

BUH BYE

As Jax and his escort entered the hangar bay, he saw his friends boarding the same transport they'd arrived on. "Hey, guys!" he shouted. He turned to the ensign escorting him, who had steadfastly resisted his flirtations during their walk from interrogation to the flight deck. "I think I got it from here." She stopped walking and nodded. The look on her face revealed how relieved she was to be free of his attentions.

Jax stepped aboard the shuttle a second before the ramp raised. Everyone was accounted for, plus four shock troopers. "Hi, guys." He waved as he dropped into the jump seat next to Naomi. He leaned over, whispering, "You have something to do with this?" He wiggled his fingers to make sure she knew what he meant.

She looked around, paying particular attention to the shock troops watching over them. After running her hands through her jet-black hair, she whispered, "Yeah. They put us in a conference room with a terminal they thought was locked down."

Jax made a face. "What? I was in a shitty interrogation room."

"There were wraps: veggie and shawarma," she added.

"The fuck?" Jax turned to look at Kori and Steve. "You had wraps?" Both of them nodded. "I had to beg for a hamburger." He smiled wistfully, remembering the juicy patty. "It was good, though." He closed his eyes.

Kori sighed. "So, what's going on? No one told us anything."

Jax related his discussions with the captain and what their release likely meant. The entire time the shock troop escorts never said a word, their armored boots holding them to the deck as the shuttle bounced and rocked.

"Hey, look." Steve pointed out one of the windows. Three shuttles similar to the one they were in were rocketing away from the planet toward the Imperial vessel.

The moment Jax stepped off the troop transport's ramp, it rose, nearly knocking him over. The powerful lift engines cycled up, blasting all four of them with dirt. As the transport rose, Jax raised both hands, middle fingers extended. He turned and looked at the others. "Assholes." He pointed to the *Osprey,* still sitting where Skip had landed her a few hours ago.

As they approached the Valerian Co-op Infiltrator, its exterior lights flicked on, bathing the surrounding area in light. From the external speakers, Skip said, "Welcome home."

Jax smiled and shouted, "Good to be home." They walked up the boarding ramp to find Rudy and Baxter in the small embarkation room, which made the space incredibly crowded.

The combat droid nodded his head. "Glad you all made it back. Those Imperial goons were annoying."

The group made their way up the stairs, through the cargo hold, and into the common area. Rudy shot up the center of the staircase all the way to the bridge. Jax followed. "I'll get us underway."

Kori said, "We're behind schedule. Think you can swing by Jericho?"

Jax leaned down to peek below the threshold of the ceiling. "Yeah, I've nothing booked." He looked at Steve. "You cool with that?" The other man nodded. He stood up.

"Hey, you didn't ask me?" Naomi protested.

From the flight deck, Jax shouted, "You're technically still a stowaway."

Naomi looked at Steve, then Kori. "Rude," she muttered.

SIXTEEN

JERICHO STATION

The trip from Jebidiah to Jericho Station wasn't too long. Jax and the others occupied their time watching various old-time vids, and until they ran out of beer, getting drunk. Despite the overall failure of the job, doing the right thing and surviving more than one Imperial entanglement were enough to keep their collective spirits up. It helped that all the room swapping and awkwardness of their earlier trip was over, so everyone could get a better night's sleep.

Jericho station was a very different design from Kelso. Where Kelso was basically a cigar stuck through a donut, Jericho was three times the size and basically a dumbbell, two spheres nearly half a kilometer in diameter connected by a kilometer long and three-hundred-meter-wide central span.

The *Osprey* had been given docking clearance in what Kori told them was the low-rent docking area in Sphere One. Her boss, she further explained, would be docking in the other sphere in less than an hour. Jax and Steve promised to have Marshall ship the rest of her luggage from Kelso.

As the group descended the boarding ramp, Jax looked at Kori, duffel bag slung over her shoulder. "Don't be a stranger."

Steve hugged her and said, "My brother is gonna be pissed." He looked sidelong at Jax. "I'm gonna send him his way." He hitched a thumb.

Kori nodded, smiling. "I commed Marshall last night and let him know." She looked at Jax. "He's still pissed and definitely has plans for you when you all get to Kelso, though." Jax shuddered. She turned to Naomi. "It was nice to meet you, Naomi. I hope you and Jax figure out a business arrangement."

The Japanese woman grinned. "Oh, that's all settled."

"It is?" Jax turned. Naomi just smiled.

"Well, I gotta jet. Stay safe. I'm pretty sure you," pointing at Jax, "haven't seen the last of the Crimson Orchid. Hopefully that Ichiko guy doesn't remember the rest of our names."

Naomi wanted to do some digging from a computer network that wasn't Kelso, so while she and Rudy worked, Jax and Steve went off in search of dinner and supplies.

The two men were finishing a pre-taking-dinner-back-to-Naomi beer when Jax's gPhone buzzed. He took it out and when he saw the screen made a face, holding the device out for Steve to see the screen. NO-IDENT blinked across the screen. "Crimson Orchid?" Jax guessed.

Steve nodded slowly. "Or someone trying to sell you real estate on New Terra."

Jax pressed the ACCEPT icon. "Hello, Mr. Caruso. Oh, and you, too, Mr. Delphino." His grin was not friendly.

So much for the *not remembering the last names of the others,* thing. It was Ichiko. "I just wanted you to know that you've made very powerful enemies in the Crimson Orchid."

Jax shrugged. "Well, you were planning to kill us instead of paying the remaining thirty percent on the job, so you know, I kinda see us as even."

"Oh, no," the older man said, his smile very much unfriendly. "We are anything but. I only just avoided the authorities on Themura. Many of my lieutenants did not. No, Mr. Caruso, we are not even."

This time it was Steve who replied. "Yeah, well, sounds like you're not in much of a position to do anything about it." He offered his fist to Jax outside the view of the phone's camera pickup. Jax bumped his own fist against it.

"For now, yes. I just thought you should know that our dealings are not concluded." Again, the older man smiled a wicked smile. "Remember, we know where you live."

Jax's face went flat. "You do, and you should remember how easy it was to get the Imps on your ass." He winked. "Something to think about." He ended the call.

Steve looked at him. "You're an idiot."

"So, a second chance is out of the question?" Jax asked as he finished his beer. He flagged down their server. "We're ready to go if our food is."

She nodded. "I'll go get it."

Steve hadn't moved, but when Jax looked back to him, he smiled. "Not a chance in hell. What was it Naomi said? This," he pointed at himself, then Jax, then himself again, "is never gonna happen." He paused. "Well, again." He slapped Jax's knee. "I'll wait outside." He stood and headed for the door.

Jax laughed, watching someone he hoped was his friend

walk out. "Probably a smart choice." The server brought the to-go order and checked Jax out.

He thumbed his gPhone. "Naomi, we're on our way back. Have Rudy and Skip get ready for departure."

"Roger that, partner," the woman replied. Jax made a face but said nothing. She added, "Let's go home."

The end.

CONTINUE THE ADVENTURE

If you enjoyed this story, I'd love it if you left a review.
Seriously, reviews are a big deal.
Reviews help readers find authors.
Even just "I liked it" means a lot!

The second book in the Grand Human Empire series, 'Side Hustle Tango' comes out May, 27th.
Get your copy now!

This is but the first adventure of Jax, Naomi and the droids. I loved writing it and seeing these characters come alive on the page. There's so much more to come for all of them, I can't wait to share with you!

Want to stay up to date on the happenings in the Grand Human Empire?

Sign up for my newsletter at
johnwilker.com/newsletter
Visit me online at
johnwilker.com
You can also join my Patreon page for all
sorts of awesome goodies!

If you like supporting things you love by sporting merch or buying direct, well you're in luck! I've launched a shop, take a look. **Use, discount code "Osprey" and you'll save %15!**

OFFER

As they say, there's no harm in asking, so here we go.

If you can help connect me with someone who can get The Grand human Empire on a screen (Big or Little) I'll cut you in for 10% (Up to $10,000) of whatever advance is paid.

Send me an email and we can discuss.
rights@johnwilker.com

ABOUT ME

I've loved writing since I was a kid. I entered writing contests in 2nd and 3rd grade (won one, lost one). I read books and wrote book reports for my parents (It helped that I got a new G.I. Joe for each book report). From that point on I've told stories wherever I could.

I used to send a weekly email to coworkers letting them know we had donuts. Each one was a story. Folks signed up just to read the stories (leaving more donuts for me!).

I hope to keep telling the stories for as long as people enjoy reading them.

Tell your friends, tell your family, tell the person next to you on the plane that just looked at you funny for laughing out loud. You see where I'm going with this. :)